TO THE RESCUE

Dex looked around. A discarded singletree with one end broken off lay at the base of the mud wall close to the gate. Dex picked that up and weighed it in his hand.

He stepped quietly behind the man who was groping Selma, took a comfortable stance . . . and whaled the bejabbers out of the big SOB.

From behind. Without warning. Hard.

The singletree hit the back of the man's head with a sound like a melon being thumped, and the fellow dropped dead away taking Selma down to the ground with him.

With a shrug, Dex took a fresh grip on his trusty singletree and went stalking another scalp for his trophy belt.

When he was within three or four paces of Ben, the piece of dumb muscle who was holding the kid noticed Dex's presence and signified the arrival of company by croaking a sound of warning.

Ben whirled, leather strap raised ready to strike. Dex would've bet his last dollar on the idea that good old Ben was expecting to see Selma coming at his backside. The man was not prepared to face a grown man instead.

"Surprise," Dex said.

And smashed Ben over the head with the singletree . . .

DIAMONDBACK

MADE IN SPADES

♦ ♦ ♦

Guy Brewer

JOVE BOOKS, NEW YORK

This is a work of fiction. Names, characters, places, and incidents are either the product of the author's imagination or are used fictitiously, and any resemblance to actual persons, living or dead, business establishments, events, or locales is entirely coincidental.

MADE IN SPADES

A Jove Book / published by arrangement with
the author

PRINTING HISTORY
Jove edition / November 2000

The Penguin Putnam Inc. World Wide Web site address is
http://www.penguinputnam.com

ISBN: 0-515-12955-0

A JOVE BOOK®
Jove Books are published by The Berkley Publishing Group,
a division of Penguin Putnam Inc.,
375 Hudson Street, New York, New York 10014.
JOVE and the "J" design
are trademarks belonging to Penguin Putnam Inc.

PRINTED IN THE UNITED STATES OF AMERICA

10 9 8 7 6 5 4 3 2 1

• 1 •

His first conscious thought was that he was horny. He had a raging early morning hard-on and he wasn't even sure it was morning. Could still be the middle of the night for all he knew as there wasn't a hint of rosy pink dawn light showing around the edges of the pull-down blind. But horny? He was sure of that. He was so hard it ached and was going bumpity bump in time with his heartbeat, bouncing off his belly with each fresh pulse and demanding relief.

Dex rolled onto his side and touched the waist of the naked girl who was asleep beside him. She was a cute little morsel. Slim and brown, with waist-length black hair and skin that had a faintly yeasty flavor. Didn't seem to speak a word of English. But then she didn't have to. Her hands and eyes and lips—and certain select other parts as well—more than made up for any shortcomings in the conventional forms of communication.

Dex's pecker practically stood up and begged in response to the feel of her flesh. And if it didn't exactly beg, well, it damn sure stood up. He wasn't in any confusion as to what the insistent member had in mind.

"Psst. Hey. Puta," he whispered. Puta being the name she'd given him when she tried to introduce herself last night. She'd quickly learned that Dexter had no more Spanish than she was possessed of English, so she'd settled for pointing to herself and saying "Puta" a couple of times. That, coupled with a wink and a huge smile and a nod across the street toward the hotel had been enough to convince him.

She was a pretty little thing, no doubt about it. She had a wide mouth with full, puffy lips. Eyes big enough to bathe in and hair that was cool and silky when dragged teasingly over a man's naked body.

"Psst. Wake up, honey."

The girl stirred and muttered a little in her sleep, and Dex moved closer to her, fitting his own lean frame tight against hers like a pair of spoons nested one inside the other.

His pecker lay trapped between the cheeks of her round little butt, but she didn't wake up. Dex reached across her body to stroke her belly and toy with the curling hair of her bush—thick and glossy stuff, as he well remembered from close and frequent inspection last night—but he couldn't reach the plump lips of her pussy because she was lying on her side with her thighs pressed tightly together.

He settled for running his hand over the flat of her belly and onto her tit. He had no idea how old Puta was, but there was no doubt she was young enough that her tits were still as hard as unripe pears. And damn near as pointy too. They were perky and firm, standing proud with very dark, sharp-tipped nipples set onto that dusky brown flesh.

Puta sniffed loudly and mumbled something that he wouldn't have been able to understand even if he'd heard it.

He squeezed her left tit—the right one was pressed tight against the mattress so he couldn't reach it very well—but still she didn't waken.

Dex pushed himself tighter against her backside, hoping she would feel the immediacy of his need and waken. But she didn't.

If he didn't manage to get inside that sweet little honeybox she carried between her legs he was gonna burst. He knew without doubt that something inside him would purely swell beyond the capacity of mortal flesh to endure, and he would injure himself when the pressure blew his insides clean apart.

If he didn't have Puta and have her right damn now he was just gonna die. Or something.

He tried again. Whispered. Squeezed. Shook and stroked her. The damned girl slept peacefully on.

Dex's poor, denied pecker wasn't going to be able to take this much longer, dammit.

He squirmed and wriggled in his discomfort. And in his desire to communicate something of this need to the unconscious and unresponsive girl who lay so tantalizingly near and yet so sleepily distant.

"Oh, hell," he muttered, sure he was going to drench her ass with a flood of sticky semen if he didn't get in there soon.

With a grimace and a sigh, Dex decided to take things into his own hands.

Not literally though. Not with a pretty girl like Puta right there to receive him.

He reached down and slid his hand between her legs, lifting a little to raise her left leg . . . just enough to . . . ah, there!

Dex's cat-couldn't-scratch-it hard-on found its way home.

He arched his back and angled his pelvis forward, and his pecker glided happily into the hot, sweet depths.

That was more like it.

Dex cupped his hand around Puta's left tit and began stroking back and forth, slowly at first and then with greater and greater urgency.

Not, he reflected, an entirely bad way for a gent to waken.

◆ 2 ◆

Dex stroked the back of Puta's head, smoothing down the rumpled pelt of black hair. Ah, she was a sweetie, all right. She could take everything he had—something not every girl was capable of handling—and even managed to stuff most of his length down her throat. Which she was obediently doing now.

Beat hell out of getting up and washing the juices off in cold water any old time, Dex thought.

Dex pulled the pretty girl off him, certain she would have been willing to stay there until he either came again or his prick wore down to a bloody nub, whichever he desired.

What he desired right now, though, was breakfast. He'd been enjoying Puta for the past couple hours, one way and another, and now he was hungry enough to eat her. Which in itself was not an entirely unpleasant thought if not one to be undertaken until he'd put a solid meal behind his belt buckle.

"That's enough, honey," he said. The words made no impression but a gentle lift of his fingers beneath her chin did. She let his slick and slippery length slip out past her lips and looked up at him with a wide, happy smile.

"Are you hungry?" he asked.

Predictably, Puta did not respond to the question so he mimed eating. That suggestion made her smile all the bigger.

"Let's get dressed and I'll buy you some breakfast," he said and proceeded to demonstrate.

Dex padded naked over to the hotel room mirror and used his comb and brushes to tidy himself before dressing.

He was not particularly impressed by what he saw in any mirror, but his great good fortune was that a clear majority of available females seemed to like the outward appearances of Dexter Lee Yancey, late of Louisiana and more recently a gentleman of no permanent address.

Leaving home had seemed . . . well . . . advisable at the time. Courts and charges and prison terms had been mentioned. That was some months past, and Dex had discovered that he enjoyed the adventures and the challenges of travel.

He stood now in a small but nicely maintained hotel on the town plaza of Huaca Guadalupe, New Mexico Territory, and inspected himself closely.

Just shy of six feet in height and in his late twenties with a lean and muscular build, Dex had dark blond hair and Burnside whiskers sweeping down to the shelf of his jaw. He had brown eyes and delicately made hands, the fingers long and slender.

He combed out his whiskers and wet his hair before brushing it back to quell the licks and tangles of the night, then quickly dressed in light gray trousers, black stovepipe books, a dark gray swallowtail coat, and a low crowned pearl gray planter's hat. The cravat he chose for the day was a bright and cheerful yellow. But then Dex himself was a bright and cheerful fellow.

He strapped on a pair of stubby, sturdy, British-made Webley revolvers in .455 caliber, one positioned to the left of his buckle in a crossdraw holster and the other tucked rather less conspicuously into the small of his back where it was hidden by his coat.

He also customarily carried a walking stick with a Malacca barrel and eagle's head handgrip. Within the barrel was a thin but very sharp and flexible blade of Toledo steel.

He had been raised as a gentleman in the traditions of the south, and his education included formal schooling and all the other accomplishments customary to his class. He could ride, fence, shoot, gamble, drink, and cut swaths through the ladies with the best of them.

What he could not do was fit into an ordinary and humdrum workaday world.

Since leaving his plantation home, however, he had discovered that he did possess certain talents that might yet make it possible for him to survive, even to prosper.

At the moment, fortunately, his pockets were nicely heavy.

And thinking of which, he dipped into one and extracted a five dollar gold half eagle coin which he handed to Puta with a smile and a flourish, well aware that the girl likely would have been satisfied with fifty cents, pleased with a dollar and ecstatic with two. She had pleased him, and now he wanted to buy her breakfast in addition to the munificent fee.

Once in the hallway he held up a finger asking her to

wait, then tapped lightly on the door to the room next door. The response was quick. "Don't crap yourself. I'll be right out."

Seconds later the door opened and a tall—a mere half inch taller than Dex, although the individual in question made much of that small difference—Negro stepped out to join them.

James had been Dex's best friend for as long as either of them could remember. Once he had also been Dex's slave, a living playtoy intended to serve and to amuse. What no one but the two of them ever recognized, however, was that their true relationship had been one of deep friendship virtually from the beginning.

Friends they had been and friends they still were.

"Hello, young miss," James said, every bit as gallantly as Dex might have. But then something else no one but the two of them seemed to recognize in the past was the fact that while James appeared only to serve, he also learned. His manners, his education, his abilities were as complete as were Dexter's. Now he bowed to the pretty girl and received a smile from her in return. She said something in Spanish. Unfortunately James knew no more Spanish than Dex did so her pleasantry, if such it was, proved to be wasted.

"Where's your girl?" Dex asked.

James frowned and shrugged. "She wasn't near as nice as she looked. I sent her home before daybreak."

"Hungry?"

"I could eat a horse."

"Careful what you say," Dex advised. "Could be that we will. And never know it."

"As long as I don't know it then I expect it will be all right."

Dex offered Puta his arm and led the way downstairs and out into the bright light of a lovely New Mexico day.

The café was pleasant enough. A decrepit little daub-and-wattle house served as the kitchen and, for all Dex knew, the residence of the fat Mexican and his even fatter wife who ran the place. An arbor had been built over a stone-paved patio and furnished with tables and stools. Grape vines hanging heavy with as yet unripe fruit served as a sort of roof to provide shade. Apparently people in this country worried little about protecting themselves from rain. But then a long look around would show there was too little of that to bother considering. It was obviously a dry land.

The alfresco dining arrangement might have reminded Dex of New Orleans, a city which he remembered fondly from many visits. It did not. There was a rather wide gap between Huaca Guadalupe and New Orleans, a gap much broader than mere miles would suggest.

Still, Huaca Guadalupe was what they had so Huaca Guadalupe was what they would enjoy.

Dex led the way to one of the very few empty tables and motioned for the proprietor to join them.

"Do you speak English?"

"Si, señor."

"My friend and I will have beefsteak and potatoes. We'll want the potatoes sliced thin and fried crisp and brown. You understand?"

Dex waited for a response and after a moment the Mexican nodded and smiled. "Si, señor."

"Coffee of course. And some biscuits. We'd like a big plate of biscuits. And bring Puta whatever she wants, too." He nodded toward the girl.

The Mexican gave Dex a look that seemed decidedly strange. And more than a little hostile. For a moment Dex thought the man was going to explode into a rage.

The girl—in daylight she looked prettier and perhaps even younger than he'd thought—burst into a gush of liquid words. The restaurateur responded with another. Dex wasn't sure if the two of them were discussing breakfast or reciting their family lineages. Whatever they were talking about seemed to take an awfully long time. And whatever it was also served to calm the Mexican. His brief flare of hostility dissolved into a polite, if distant, indifference.

That was just fine by Dex. All he wanted was a meal. He had no interest in making friends here anyway. An hour or so to eat and collect their gear and horses and he and James would be moving on.

Besides this was a delightful morning, the day's heat not yet oppressive, the sky clear, the air clean and fresh. They were in no hurry. Eventually Puta and the Mexican concluded their conversation and the man left.

Dex smiled at Puta and was about to say something

when a man at the adjacent table stood and moved closer to stand scowling down at Dexter. He too had a belligerent look about him.

Dex stood. If the SOB wanted to start something—

"You didn't have to shame her," the man said in an accusing tone.

"Shame who? What the hell are you talking about, mister?" At least this man was an American. Or what they seemed to refer to around here as an Anglo. He spoke English.

The fellow looked down at Puta and nodded. "The girl, of course. You shouldn't have shamed her like that. She's a nice girl. I know her family, and they're respectable people. You might think she's only a toy for you to abuse, but she has feelings. You insult her like this, right out here in public, she'll likely never get over the shame of it. It's a lousy thing you've done to her, and she doesn't deserve it."

Dex frowned. "Shamed who? You mean Puta?"

The man—he wasn't an imposing sort, seemed quite decent in fact—grabbed Dex by the lapels of his coat and shoved his face nose-to-nose with him. "I told you, dammit, quit that."

Dex was aware that on the other side of the table James moved his stool back a little, freeing his hands in case he had to go for the twin .32 revolvers he carried out of sight.

"Mister, what in hell are you talking about?"

"The girl," the man snapped.

"Puta?"

The man let go of Dex's coat and punched him instead. He was quicker than Dex expected.

And he threw one hell of a fine right hand.

Dex took the first one, ducked underneath the second and got around to the business of defending himself from this baffling onslaught.

• 4 •

"Had enough, have you? Are you gonna apologize now?"

Dex shook his head—it seemed a bit fuzzy at the moment—and picked himself up off the sandstone paving blocks. For the third time. Or maybe it was the fourth. He wasn't exactly sure which.

He'd encountered damn few men who could best him in the arts and pleasures of gentlemanly fisticuffs. This man could. Dammit.

Still, Dex was not a quitter. Give him a couple seconds to clear his head and get his breath . . . he'd go it again. He shook his head and noticed a thin spray of bright red droplets land on the table where this oddly combative fellow had been eating. Good. If Dex couldn't beat the son of a bitch maybe he could ruin the guy's breakfast anyway.

Funny, but that seemed small comfort at the moment.

"Well?" the man demanded.

"Apologize for *what*?" Dex bleated in exasperation. "What the hell am I supposed to've done?"

"What have you done? You step in here and destroy that child's reputation and then you have the audacity to act like you've done nothing wrong?"

"I suppose you mean Puta since she's the only girl I've talked with or about in this place, but . . . dammit, will you leave be your boxing for a minute and let me be clear about this?"

The fellow dropped his hands and stepped back half a pace. He was ready to come again though. Dex could see that clear enough.

"I don't know what you're talking about," Dex insisted.

"You call her a whore, in public, and you don't have sense enough to know that you shouldn't have?" the man snapped.

"Call her what? I haven't said a word about any such. All I've done is want to buy her breakfast. What's so insulting about that?"

"Puta," the man said in a low voice.

"Exactly," Dex said. "What about her?"

"The word."

"What word?"

"Puta."

"Look, are we going to run in circles about this? Puta's a nice girl. I like her. I wouldn't do anything in the world to hurt her. Now can I—"

"Whoa," the fellow said.

"Whoa what?"

"Don't you know?"

"Mister, I don't have any least idea what you are talking about. And if I don't know something then, well, I wouldn't know that I don't know it. If that makes sense.

Which I suppose it doesn't. But the fact remains. I don't know who you are or what this is all about, but I can assure you that I would never, under any circumstances, say or do anything that I thought could reflect badly on Puta."

"Sweet Jesus," the Anglo said. "You thought—"

The man turned and in a very loud voice, more than loud enough to reach the ears of everyone in and around the cafe, launched into a long spiel in Spanish.

While he was doing that Dex looked across the table at James and whispered, "Big help you've been."

James grinned at him. "Hell, white boy, there's only one of him. What do you need me for?"

Dex rubbed his chin—his vision was still a little blurry—and tried to wipe some of the blood off his face with a table napkin. The damned Anglo was fast with his hands, damn him, and knew how to use his speed to best effect, too.

After several minutes and what seemed like a brief question and answer session amongst the diners, the Anglo turned back to Dex. "I explained to them what happened."

"Well I wish to hell you'd explain it to me. I still don't have a clue," Dex told him.

The man grinned a little. But then he could. He'd hardly been touched during the fracas. "The girl's name is Anselma. She's usually called Selma."

"But I thought—"

"Puta is a word, mister. It means 'whore'."

"Oh, shit," Dex blurted.

"Exactly," the Anglo agreed.

"What I told everybody is that when she met you and tried to explain to you that she was not a prostitute she used that word and you misunderstood and thought she was telling you that it was her name." The fellow paused. "I also told them that the only thing between you and her is breakfast. I didn't try to explain just why you would want to buy breakfast for a girl you can't even speak with. No point in raising questions unnecessarily, if you see what I mean."

"Jesus, I . . . I'd never want to hurt her. She's sweet. Selma, you say her name is?"

The Anglo nodded.

Dex turned and tried to give the weeping girl an apology. But of course he did not have the words. Literally did not. And even if he'd known any Spanish, at this moment he could think of nothing he could possibly say that would compensate for the hurt he'd so unintentionally inflicted upon her. "I . . . I don't—" Nothing would come out.

"You really didn't know, did you? You really didn't want to hurt her," the Anglo said.

"No. Never."

"I'll speak with her," he offered. He took the stool Dex had vacated and for some minutes spoke in low, earnest tones to her, eliciting nods from the pretty girl and eventually even a hesitant smile or two. When he was done he said something in parting and stood, turning back to Dexter again.

"If you don't mind, mister, Selma appreciates your offer of a meal but thinks she would like to go home now."

Dex went to her side and bowed, very low, very formal. He took her hand and assisted her to her feet with all the courtesy he would have given the finest belle of the South.

Selma said something in a soft voice, then turned and

fled, walking until she was out of the café arbor and then breaking into a girlish run.

Dex turned back to thank the Anglo he'd just been fighting with, but the man was gone.

"He slipped out that way," James said, nodding toward the back of the patio.

Dex rubbed the side of his face. The merciful numbness that kept a person from feeling his wounds while receiving them was fading now, and he was beginning to hurt like crazy. He suspected that was something that would get even worse before it began to get better.

But he'd earned these bruises, dammit. He felt like nine kinds of an ass for causing such a problem for such a sweet and cheerful girl.

The Mexican café owner came out bearing a tray with breakfast enough for four, never mind the three who'd originally ordered.

The café owner, Dex discovered, apparently had no more English than Selma did because on the tray there was not even a hint of beefsteak, potatoes, or biscuits. Instead it seemed they would be having what apparently served here as a grand breakfast. Spicy beans. Hot corn tortillas. Peppers, cucumbers, and sliced onion swimming in vinegar. And a lump of goat cheese. No meat. Dex sighed.

"Looks, uh, wonderful," James said, the sarcasm thick in his voice.

"I think we're probably lucky to get anything at all," Dex suggested.

"You have a point there, white boy."

"Eat up. I don't know about you but I'll be happy to

see the other side of this town and put it far, far behind us."

James grunted and dug a spoon into the huge serving of chili-spiced red beans.

• 5 •

Dex finished rolling and tying his spare clothing into a sausagelike roll that was protected with a square of oil-cloth and carried behind his cantle. He tossed the bundle onto the unmade hotel room bed next to his saddlebags, then turned to James.

"What are you looking so sad about?" Dex asked. "I'm the one got beat up. All you did was cheer. And I'm not even sure which one of us you were cheering for."

James sank down onto the lone chair in the room. He had already done his packing and brought his gear with him to Dex's room. "I want to have a word with you, Dex."

Dex frowned. "This sounds serious."

"It is," James confessed.

"All right then. Let's talk." Dex settled onto the side of the bed next to his things.

"You know I been thinking an awful lot lately about mama."

"I know you have, James."

"Dexter, I wanta go home and see her again. She's not . . . far as I know her health is fine. But a person never knows. I'd hate to learn someday that she's died and I never got to hug her again or eat her cooking and listen to her humming in the mornings while she puts the biscuit dough out to raise. You know what I mean?"

"I think I do." Dex never knew his own mother. James's mother had filled that role for him when he and James were growing up and James's mother was the cook in the Yancey family kitchen.

"I want to go home for a spell, Dex. I want to see mama again. I want to walk down by that ol' Mississippi and catch me a catfish. I want to see the home place one more time."

Dex nodded. "I can understand that."

"I know you do. And I know you can't go back. Wouldn't be safe for you to show yourself anywhere near Blackgum Bend or the crossing. Lewis'd have you jailed quick as he saw you."

"I expect he would at that." Lewis Yancey was Dex's very slightly younger twin brother. It was Lewis's lies and manipulations that kept Dex from inheriting the plantation when their father died and as is so often the case in life, it was the transgressor—perhaps due to his own sense of guilt—who harbored hatred for his own victim and not the other way around. Lewis despised and very likely feared Dexter. Dex doubted that would ever change.

"I want to ride back alone, Dex. I . . . I feel the need. You know what I'm saying?"

"I know. I understand." Dex smiled. "I'll miss you, you ugly black son of a bitch."

"White damned ofay bastard."

Dex grinned. "Niggerboy."

"Needledick bugfucker."

They both laughed. There had been a time, back when they were ten or eleven, when trading insults had been the only way they knew to show their affection to one another. Sometimes it still was.

"I really will miss you, you know," Dex said.

"Yeah. Me, too." James stood and began unbuttoning his trousers.

"I said I'd miss you, asshole. I didn't say I wanted to go *that* far with it."

"The money belt, idiot. I have to open my britches to get to the money belt." James normally wore the belt with their cache of cash in it, this on the theory that if anyone were to rob them they would expect a white gentleman to have money but would be much less apt to think his black "servant" worth robbing.

"How much do we have in there?" Dex asked.

James shrugged. "I haven't counted it lately. Call it, oh, seventeen hundred or so."

"Give me, let's say five hundred out of that. You take the rest."

"But—"

"No, don't argue with me now. Take it to your mama and tell her I love her."

James thought about that for only a moment before he nodded. It was the right thing to do and both of them knew it.

"Will you be coming back west?" Dex asked.

"I expect I will. Bye and bye."

"If it's any time soon, say before the end of this year, look for me in Santa Fe. I've heard a lot about that old city. I want to get around to seeing it."

"And after that?"

Dex shrugged. "I'm not sure. Denver, maybe. It sounds interesting. Or San Francisco."

James chucked. "Sure. After all, they're practically next door."

"You'll find me if you look."

"I expect I'll look if I decide to come back out. Is there any message you want to send to . . . anyone?"

Dex shook his head. "Just to your mama. No one else." There had been girls but . . . no one who really counted. It struck him as odd now that he thought about it, but there really was no one back home in Louisiana who he cared all that much about. Except James and his mother. There was no one else.

Back home. It didn't seem like much of a home when he thought about it like that. He wondered where his "home" was now. Or if he would ever really have one again.

They sat in silence for some minutes. Then with a pro-longed sigh, James stood.

"It's time," he said.

Dex nodded. He stood too and was still for a moment looking into James's chocolate-hued face.

There was much Dex thought about saying. But he did not.

Finally, mutely, he stepped forward and gave James a bearhug. "Ugly fucking nigger boy."

"Ignorant damn ofay." James looked like he was hold-ing back tears. But then, hell, so was Dex.

"You take care."

"Yeah, you, too."

James picked up his saddlebags and clothing roll. "You coming?"

Dex shook his head. "Not yet a while."

"All right. I, uh, I—"

"I'll see you later, okay?"

"Yeah. Later." James turned and left, moving in a stiff and hurried gait. He hadn't any more than shut the hotel room door than Dex was missing him. If Dex caught up with him, asked him to stay, James would stay. Dex knew that. But it wouldn't be fair. Dex remained where he was. He heard James's footsteps on the bare wooden stairs.

Then nothing.

Dex dropped into an uncomfortable seat on the edge of the bed. He supposed he should get up and go on about his business.

But he just damned well didn't feel like it. Later maybe but not right now.

✦ 6 ✦

His teeth hurt. His mouth tasted like every alligator in Louisiana's bayous had crapped in it. His brains were probably drooling out of the fissure that was splitting his skull half in two. And those were the *best* things he could say about his condition.

He'd had—jeez, he didn't know how many drinks last night. He'd started knocking back bar whiskey and chasing it with beer. After that . . . he had no idea. Judging from the way he felt this morning he'd believe anything anyone wanted to accuse him of.

He was . . .

A singularly unpleasant thought struck him and he grabbed for his midsection. Not so much because of his bellyache—although he had one of those, too—but to see if his money belt was . . . ah!

It was there. If he'd been a praying man this probably would've been a very good time for it. What was the old saying? Something about God protecting drunks and fools. Well, in this case the divinity had been able to watch out for both of those at the same time. The proof of it was that the belt containing the entirety of his worldly wealth was still on his person.

A further thought struck him and he opened his trousers and felt of the webbed cotton belt. The bulk of folded currency was there.

Still fearful, he opened the first small pouch on the belt and withdrew the paper. It was indeed currency. No one substituted like-sized scraps of newspaper for the money he'd been carrying.

Anyone could have. It was only a blind drunk's blind luck that he hadn't been robbed.

He still had . . . he looked around. As far as he could tell he still had everything he'd arrived with.

Assuming he was still in Huaca Guadalupe. He decided to take that on faith for the time being, for two reasons. The first was that right now he really did not care where he was. The second reason was that right now there was no way Dex would trust himself to stand upright and walk over to the window. He would surely fall down and break something, more than likely himself.

He blinked and tried to get a bit of control over the spinning his room was doing, then peered owlishly about.

He was in his hotel room again. He was pretty sure about that. His clothing roll and saddlebags were still on the bed where he'd left them when he walked out yesterday morning.

He himself seemed to be on the floor beside the bed. Probably he'd slept there. He couldn't say for sure.

As to who might have brought him back here—he would have shaken his head in consternation except he didn't trust himself to survive that much movement—that was anybody's guess.

Someone surely must have brought him here. He was reasonably sure he could not have navigated the trip of his own accord.

Dex wrinkled his nose. Whoever carried him up here must have a mighty strong stomach. Dex's clothing stank, and a greenish yellow residue on his coat and shirt and trousers made it all too clear what they stank of.

Once he realized that he felt even more dreadful than before. His skin crawled as if with lice, and the thought of touching those befouled buttons on his shirt was vile.

Had to be done though. And quickly.

Dex came swaying and wobbling to his knees and then, with the support of a chair to cling to, onto his feet. He pushed the chair along toward the door, leaning on it and creeping ahead inches at a time like an especially feeble nonagenarian until he was able to reach the bell pull and give it a double tug.

"Water," he croaked when the boy finally appeared half an eternity later.

"You want a pitcher o' drinking water, mister?" the kid asked. Dex would almost have sworn the question was deliberately malicious. But then what the hell did he know. Maybe he'd done something to offend this boy last night. Like propositioning the kid's grandmother or something.

"God no," he said. "I don't want to get that started up again. I want a bath."

"There's no hot water, mister. It's all used up."

The little bastard was probably lying, Dex thought uncharitably. Fine. Let him. Never mind the small stuff. "That's all right, son. Cold water will do. I have to have a bath. And is there a dry chemical cleaner in town?"

"A what?"

"Never mind. Is there anyone here who can get clothes clean without ruining them?"

"Sure. Señora Rivera over by the—"

"That's all right. I don't have to know all the details. Just . . . bring the water, all right? I'll have my clothes bundled for you to take out."

"What if she says she can't get them clean, mister?" The boy was giving Dex's coat sleeves and the front of his soiled trousers a justifiably suspicious inspection.

"We'll cross that bridge when we get to it. And if I don't feel any better than this by then, I'll do the decent thing and throw myself off that bridge."

"Mister, you sure must've had you some fun last night."

"I'll never know," Dex said. "You, uh, don't happen to know who brought me back to my room, do you?"

"Sure. It was the Valdez brothers Pete an' Repeat."

"Are you making a joke at my expense?"

"No, sir. That's what everybody calls them. Honest. They're really—Pedro is Pete's proper name. I forget Repeat's for-sure name. Anyhow, they're the ones carried you up here."

The boy looked like he had more details to offer, but Dex wasn't so sure he wanted to hear them. "Valdez, huh?"

"Yes, sir."

He owed them, that was certain. Whoever the hell they were.

"Bring the tub in and water to fill it soon as you can, will you. I'll have the clothes ready before you're done."

"Yes, sir."

Now if he could just manage to avoid drowning in the bathwater maybe he'd survive another day.

But not to drink again. No indeed. He was off the stuff from here on. Never again. Never.

Dex contemplated the distance that lay between the door, where he now was, and the bed, where his clean clothes lay. The hell with it. He didn't need to even think about a trip of that magnitude until he was bathed and clean enough to be in the same county as those clothes anyway.

He sank gratefully onto the chair that had been his prop and good friend on his journey to get this far and began to strip out of the befouled and reeking clothing that was pasted all limp and clammy to his flesh.

Oh, what a wretched example of humanity Dex found himself to be at this miserable moment.

Never more. Never more.

• 7 •

Dex was torn. He was almost desperately hungry, his stomach having been emptied—repeatedly, until his toenails should have been dredged up from the depths of his body—yet the mere thought of food, any sort of food, was enough to make him want to puke again.

He thought it over and decided he would risk the intake of a mouthful of something bland, then take it from there depending on his ability to keep that first bit down.

At least he'd already taken the first few steps toward recovery. He was clean. And last night's reeking clothes had been carried away so Senora Rivera could perform the magic required to make them fit for continued wear.

Dex dressed slowly. It wasn't that he was dawdling. Just that at the moment he found himself incapable of speed. Anything more than a snail's pace threatened to unbalance him and topple him onto his nose or something.

He still had his Webleys and walking stick, but with no coat to hide the revolver he normally wore in the small of his back he thought it inadvisable to carry the second one with him. He tucked it inside his now depleted clothing roll instead.

He didn't expect to need a firearm here anyway. If there were brigands or, worse, assassins hired by that blonde Texas she-fiend Jane Carter—damned woman had put a price on his head, and after all he'd done to please her, too—they could have collected his scalp at their leisure last night. No, he was sure he would find no dangers to worry about in this vicinity.

Dex made his way downstairs with great care and for once actually employed his cane as a genuine walking stick instead of wanting it for the sword it contained.

He received a surprise when he stepped outside.

Either Huaca Guadalupe had spun one hundred eighty degrees around while Dex wasn't paying attention . . . or this Day After was already nearly ended. The sun was close to the horizon Dex was positive was westward the last he knew, and it was sinking fast.

So much for breakfast. Supper would have to do.

Food. The thought was enough to make his stomach gurgle and lurch in equal measures of eagerness and revulsion.

But oh, he did truly, truly hope he could find a source for plain, ordinary, unexciting American style food this evening.

Another serving of spicy, greasy Mexican food would do him in. He might as well call for an undertaker and have himself measured for a box as face chili peppers and corn tortillas tonight.

The mere thought was enough to make him belch, and the aftertaste in his mouth very nearly put him off the thought of food again until morning.

Still, a man does what a man has to do. And in this case Dex had to go about the business of becoming halfway human again.

He squared his shoulders and marched—limped—resolutely onward into the lengthening shadows along Huaca Guadalupe's main street.

◆ 8 ◆

"Toasted bread," he ordered. "Dry. No butter or jam. And some mashed potatoes. Don't put anything on them either."

"Si, señor." The fat Mexican café owner smiled and bobbed his head and went away. Dex had no idea if the man understood a word he'd said.

He was back at the same café, that bustling emporium of spices and grease and probably greasy spices, too, for all Dex knew. He had returned here for the simple reason that he could find no other eatery in the whole of Huaca Guadalupe.

There were at least five cantinas in the town. He was sure of that many and suspected there might well be more. But only the lone café.

As for the other businesses, he hadn't bothered to pay particular attention to them but so far he'd not noticed any that dealt in foodstuffs as a specialty. No greengrocer or butcher or baker or, anyway, none that he'd noticed.

The principal commodity of trade here seemed to consist largely of liquor and of some rather smelly bales that from a distance looked like the cotton he was long familiar with from back home except bundled in smaller units.

He hadn't seen any fields planted to cotton nearby, but he supposed they could be somewhere else. Would in fact almost have to be somewhere else since the immediate vicinity was much too dry for the production of cotton crops, he was sure.

Dex was nowhere near the planter his father had been. In truth he wasn't close to equaling his bone-mean and butt-ugly brother Lewis either when it came to farming. But he was reasonably sure that after growing up on a cotton plantation he would have recognized a cotton plant if he stumbled over one and knew at least a little about its production.

He was not so curious about the bales though that he would walk out of his way to inspect these. Tomorrow maybe but definitely not tonight. Tonight he considered it something of an accomplishment to get from the hotel to the café without taking a tumble.

He looked around for a friendly face and, seeing none, settled in to wait for what he hoped would be a dry and inoffensive meal.

"Señor."

Dex turned his head to see an elderly Mexican gentleman wearing a suit that looked even older than the man himself. The old fellow was thin as a rack of bones and had snow white hair and an enormous, drooping mustache. His skin looked like old leather, brown and wrinkled, and his teeth were as yellow as a whiskey drummer's suspenders.

The old boy wore a funny-looking hat with a brim

spread about three feet across and a tall, conical peak in its crown. The brim turned up in the back and drooped low in the front and was set with tiny silver disks and a swooping design done in silver thread.

Dex thought at first the ancient was making a joke of some sort by the way he costumed himself, but his expression was much too solemn for that to be possible.

"Señor," the old man repeated softly.

"Yes?" Dex rose and bowed slightly from the waist.

"You are Señor Yancey, I believe?"

"I am. And may I have the honor of making your acquaintance, sir?"

"I believe this is yours, señor." The old man bowed too, reached into a pocket concealed inside his coat and withdrew a shiny half eagle that he held out for Dex to accept.

When Dex did not take the coin, the old man bowed again and reached around Dex to carefully but firmly place the coin onto the table beside Dex's tableware.

"Sir? I'm afraid I don't know what you—"

The old man, his face blank and his shoulders squared, bowed a final time and then turned, his back stiff as a sailor's pecker, and marched away.

"Mister. I mean, señor. Wait. I don't know—"

But he did know, Dex realized. Or sort of knew.

He could think of only one reason why an old Mexican gent, especially one of such imposing dignity, would want to give him five dollars.

But then the old man wasn't giving Dexter anything. He was returning it.

This would surely have to be the same coin he'd paid to that girl . . . Selma, was it? . . . just yesterday morning.

Who the old man might be and how he'd come into

possession of Selma's money Dex did not know.

But he was sure that he could deduce at least two facts from the old fellow's actions here. One was that the old gent's pride was at stake. The other was that he probably needed the money very badly for the girl to have done what she did in order to earn it.

Dex looked at the coin and then tucked it into his pocket. For temporary safekeeping only.

He did not bother trying to scurry after the Mexican gentleman—as if Dex were in any condition to catch him anyway—knowing that the old man's pride would not allow him to be talked out of this decision. And most certainly not in public, if ever.

Later, Dex decided. Tomorrow perhaps. In the meantime . . .

In the meantime the fat café proprietor appeared bearing Dex's supper. Corn tortillas blacked and scorched. Toasted, he guessed? And a huge mound of fried potatoes that were dripping in hot, rancid-smelling grease.

Dex's stomach did a lurching backflip, and he bolted from the table with a hand clamped hard over his mouth to keep from spewing stomach acids onto his fellow diners.

♦ 9 ♦

"Excuse me. Would you mind waiting a moment?" Dex broke into a brisk trot to catch up with one of the few people in town he could recognize. "Excuse me, please."

The gentleman, the same quick-fisted Anglo who'd knocked Dex down with such ease and impunity that morning at the café, stopped on the board sidewalk and waited.

"Yes?" His voice and expression were both tinged with doubt. But then possibly he thought Dex wanted to have another stab at fighting him.

"I apologize for bothering you, but . . . look, I'm famished and long overdue for my breakfast. Would you join me? I feel I owe you something of an apology anyway and the truth is that I'd like to ask a few questions." Dex grinned. "*Before* I shove my foot into my mouth this time."

The gent smiled and extended his hand. "Ambrose Clay," he said.

Dex introduced himself.

"I will be glad to answer any questions that I can, Mr. Yancey," Clay said. "You needn't pay for my answers."

"Actually I would enjoy the company." He laughed. "Besides, I'm hoping you will help me order something that doesn't burn all the way down. And again a day or so afterward if you know what I mean." Dex's butt was boil sore from the acid runs he'd gotten in the middle of the night last night. He would deeply appreciate a little relief from that.

"Pancho's cooking does take a little getting used to," Clay acknowledged.

"A little? More like a person would have to be born to it, I'd think."

"I believe you said you are from Louisiana, Mr. Yancey. I've had some of your Acadian dishes. They can carry a little spice, too."

"Oh, but the Cad'jun cooking is tasty, Mr. Clay. These Mexican foods are so hot the flavors are lost."

"All a matter of taste and habit I'm sure," Clay said.

While they talked they walked, ambling in the direction of the town's lone café.

Dex was more than ready for a meal now. Two nights ago he'd lost everything he had. Last night he hadn't been able to retain anything to replace that loss. Now he felt like he could eat half a beef and call it an appetizer to prepare him for the main course.

"After you, sir," Clay said when they reached the entrance to the brush arbor that served as a dining room. He motioned Dex to precede him.

"Do you have a favorite table, Mr. Clay?"

"Over there," the gentleman said. He smiled. "We're creatures of habit, are we not?"

"More than we sometimes realize." Dex waited for Clay to choose a stool in his preferred location, then sat opposite him. Dex noticed that Clay positioned himself so he could watch the rest of the diners and see out into the street as well. Ambrose Clay seemed a man who was keenly aware of the goings-on around him at all times.

"What can I help you with, Mr. Yancey?" Clay asked after the proprietor Pancho came out to take a breakfast order. The fat Mexican barely glanced in Dex's direction and seemed to accept it as a matter of course that Clay would do the ordering for both of them.

Dex explained the incident that occurred the previous evening. "I didn't want to take the old man's money," he explained now, "but I thought sure he would be offended, perhaps shamed as well, if I refused it in public. The coin almost has to be the same one I, uh, presented to Selma as a, um, gift the other day. I don't know how the old gentleman got possession of it, but I can't think of any other explanation for what he did."

"Don Cesar is Anselma's grandfather," Clay said. "He was an *hidalgo* once."

Dex raised an eyebrow.

"A gentleman of high station and breeding," Clay explained.

"That much is obvious," Dex said.

"Yes, of course. And the thought of a member of his family, especially a girl who is such a close relative," Clay shrugged, "the thought of Anselma prostituting herself would be . . . very difficult for a gentleman of the old school like Don Cesar."

"I can understand Mr. Cesar's feelings about that," Dex said.

Clay snorted and shook his head. "You know nothing

about Hispanic culture do you, Mr. Yancey?"

"How much do you know about the bayou Cajuns, Mr. Clay?" Dex countered.

Clay bowed slightly from the waist. "Point well taken. Anyway, Don is a title of sorts. Like our 'mister' but connoting a much higher degree of respect than the common 'señor' which would translate almost exactly as 'mister'."

"Uh huh."

"Cesar is his first name, not his last. His full name is Don Cesar Julio Enrico Luis Espinoza." Clay grinned. "I may have missed a few minor middle names in there, but that lot will take care of all but the most formal occasions."

"Sounds like the man has more names strung together than the Lafayette, Houston, and Pacific has railroad cars."

"It's the custom here," Clay said.

"Anyway," Dex said, "that's the situation."

"And what is it that you want to do, Mr. Yancey?"

"I want to get that little girl's money back to her. And if her family is in need maybe a little bit more to go with it."

"Trying to assuage your own conscience, Mr. Yancey? Or hers?"

"Does it matter?"

Clay shrugged again. "Perhaps not."

"Will you at least tell me where I might find the girl, please?"

"Of course," Clay said, then looked up as Pancho brought out a large round tray heaped with their breakfast.

One sniff and Dex no longer really cared if the food was highly spiced or not. Whatever it was he wanted it.

Lots of it. And quickly before his strength gave out and he fainted dead away.

"As soon as we've eaten," Clay said, "I will draw you a map. Not that I can make any claims to cartographic talents, but I trust you'll be able to find your way."

Dex was salivating so hard he had to keep swallowing to keep from drooling onto the tablecloth. There were soft boiled eggs—nothing too spicy about that—and corn fritters, hot sweet cocoa, tortillas of course, fried pork chops, crispy confections dusted with sugar and cinnamon. It was a feast and a joy. And scarcely a chili pepper in sight, at least on this table.

◆ 10 ◆

Dex glanced at the map—which despite Clay's protests that he was no cartographer looked as if it had been printed from professionally made engraving plates—and determined that, yes, this pretty much had to be the Espinoza *hacienda*.

Hacienda. Clay explained that Spanish *hacienda* was to *casa* what plantation was to house. Or pretty much so.

Dex frowned. If this layout in front of him was the New Mexico equivalent of a plantation then the Espinozas were the New Mexico equivalent of the land-poor and blood-proud families back home who'd lost everything in the war except their memories.

He could see that the place once might have been quite grand. But that was a while back. Now it was . . . seedy. Melting back into the mud it had been made from.

The buildings, and there were a good many of them, were all built from the native mud bricks he'd learned was called adobe. The thick walls were supposed to give cool shelter in summer and hold the warmth in winter. He supposed they still did. But they looked shabby now.

Even the single story sprawl of ells and wings and patios that was the central main house was falling into disrepair.

From the knoll where Dex stopped his horse before riding down to the *hacienda* he could see there were places on the roof of the house where the red clay barrel tiles had been broken or for some reason carried away and now only some gray and warping underlayment remained to turn the winter snows and the rain. If it ever rained here, that is.

Sprinkled around the main house were the outbuildings that Dex guessed would hold quarters for the hands—if any hands remained, that is—along with cookhouse, storage sheds, livestock shelters . . . something for each of the many different needs and uses that developed on a plantation or a rancho. Nearly every one of these was in a suspect state of repair, and worse off, was the adobe fence that surrounded the property like the walls of one of the mighty fortresses of old.

This fortress was mighty no more, though. Everywhere the wall was crumbling and ragged, slowly melting away a bit here and there. In several places it had been breached entirely so that a wobbly-legged colt would have no trouble picking its way through the rubble in order to escape from the hacienda.

Or, Dex thought, to gain unwanted entry.

He didn't know why the thought of enemies storming these walls came suddenly into his mind.

He shook the thought off and sternly told himself when he was in school no doubt he'd read too many fanciful tales about castles under siege and knights locked in mortal combat.

Now, seeing the dying hacienda, those stories came back to mind because of the place's resemblance to the medieval fortresses shown in his history books. That was all it was.

Even so he felt something of a chill as he took up contact with his horse's bit and urged the animal forward. A cloud must have passed over the sun to cause it.

And never mind that the day was cloudless.

• 11 •

Dex could see children. Or at least he could see selected
parts of children. Eyes, mostly. And the tops of heads. A
hand or a carelessly placed foot here. An ear and half a
face there. There were dozens of them—well, it *seemed*
like that many anyhow—every one of them intent on getting a good look at this Anglo stranger on the bay horse,
none of them brave enough to venture out into the open
to do their gawking.

Instead they huddled behind rickety wagons and around
the corners of small buildings. They peeped. They giggled. The boys among them tried to catch the little girls
unaware so as to shove them out into plain view.

Dex could see glimpses of the excitement and the
horseplay, and now and then he could even hear a whisper
of the soft noises they were making. The kids reminded
him of the way the children of the plantation hands back
home used to giggle and squirm when strangers came to

call at Blackgum Bend. Apparently kids were the same everywhere regardless of color or culture.

He stayed in the hacienda yard seated on the horse and waiting as he'd been told—by Ambrose Clay again—that it was considered impolite in this far western country for a visitor to dismount without invitation.

It took a while but eventually an adult appeared on the shaded verandah that ran along the front of the low roofed main house.

His official greeter was a middle-aged woman with graying hair done up in a tight bun and a broom carried in both hands as if she expected having to use it not for sweeping but to whack this visitor over the head. She came out into the yard to stand a few cautious paces distant from his horse and say something quite thoroughly incomprehensible to him in Spanish.

Dex removed his hat and bowed from the waist, the movement causing the horse to fidget and stamp a forefoot.

"Ma'am. I've come to pay my respects to Don Cesar." He couldn't tell if she understood or not. She only grunted and said something more to him, then turned. He wasn't positive about it but got the impression that the woman might've been a wee bit disappointed that she didn't get to hit him with her broom. She went back inside.

Dex sat where he was.

Two, three minutes later another figure appeared in the open doorway. For a split second he thought it was Anselma coming to greet him. Then the woman came out onto the verandah where he could get a better look and he saw that she was older than Anselma, although with the same striking good looks and long black hair. She was thinner than Anselma too, painfully so.

Again Dex doffed his hat. "Ma'am."

"You are Señor Yancey." It was not a question.

"Yes, ma'am."

"Please come, señor. You have ridden a long way. You should rest now and take yourself out from the sun." Her English was good, if accented. Not perfect of course but good. And a helluva lot better than his Spanish, which lay somewhere between nonexistent and none at all.

"Thank you, ma'am."

The woman's left hand moved in a vague, up-and-down gesture and instantly a teenaged boy came racing out from behind one of the many parked wagons that were in the hacienda yard—rather odd wagons with high sides, stove pipes poking out at odd angles, and roofs covered with rotting canvas—to take the reins of Dex's horse.

The boy led the bay off somewhere while Dex meekly followed the woman.

He'd expected to follow her inside the house. Instead she led him along the outer perimeter of the adobe building, down the verandah and into one of the several patios or garden courts, whatever they would be called, that he'd noticed when he saw the house from high on the knoll to the east.

She must have left instructions with someone before she walked out to greet him because there were already two glasses and a clay pitcher waiting on a round stone table that sat in the shade of a large bougainvillea.

"Lemon and honey, señor? Or I can call for something stronger if you prefer."

"This will be fine, thank you." It had been a couple days, but Dex still was of the opinion that he never wanted a drink again. Not one that contained any sort of alcohol, anyway.

"Please sit."

"Will Don Cesar be joining me here?" he asked as he settled onto a massive armchair made from some graying native wood. The three-inch thick trunk sections—cedar perhaps?—were spaced just a little too far apart so that they hurt his butt a little. Chairs like these needed cushions on them for any sort of extended sitting. He couldn't help but wonder if the oversight was intentional as a subtle means of making his visit a brief one.

The woman sat in the other of the two chairs that were provided. Dex jumped up to assist her but too late. She seemed not to notice so he sat back down again while she poured this New Mexican version of lemonade for both of them.

"Unfortunately," she said in accented English that he had to listen closely to follow, "my . . . grandfather, is it?" She lifted an eyebrow.

"Yes."

"My grandfather will not be able to receive you today. May I take with him your message?"

Dex bit back an impulse to correct her. "Please give Don Cesar my regards and tell him that I meant to give no offense to him or to any member of his family when I, uh—"

"I understand," she said, helping him over that hump of embarrassment. It would have been rather awkward for him to directly apologize for laying a member of the household. Indirection, on the other hand, was just fine.

"Thank you. I meant no ill to anyone and sincerely apologize if I inadvertently caused a . . . misunderstanding."

"I will tell my grandfather to these things."

"Thank you. May I ask if the young lady with whom

I breakfasted the other day—Anselma—she is well?"

"She is quite well, thank you."

"And you would be?" He took a sip of the lemonade. It wasn't bad. A lighter flavor than he was used to, but then a food item brought from so far away was bound to be expensive and used sparingly in this household of fading elegance. And the honey had its distinctive flavor too, sweet but not at all the same sort of sweetness given by cane sugar.

"I am Anita Espinoza Candelario. Anselma is my sister, señor."

No wonder then that he'd mistaken her for Anselma when she first appeared in the shadowed doorway. Of the two, Dex thought, Anselma was the prettier. But then she was far and away the younger as well. Anita, however, had a dignity about her and the same calm reserve that he'd noticed about her grandfather in town yesterday.

Of the two sisters it was Anita who had . . . something. That special quality that makes not a pretty girl but a genuinely beautiful woman, the sort of beauty that grows as the woman matures and remains with her even into old age. And a woman who remains handsome when she ages is a rarity to be treasured and admired.

"Your grandfather is well also?" Dex asked.

"He is, thank you. I will tell him that you ask after his health."

"I would welcome an opportunity to tell him that myself."

"Alas, señor, this cannot be."

"I see." And indeed he did. The old boy was just fine, thank you. But he was not inclined to receive upstart Anglo intruders. Especially ones that paid to fuck his granddaughter. Dex didn't blame Don Cesar actually. If anything he admired the old man for putting principle above profit.

And God knew the people who eked out a living here could use whatever stray cash came their way. The hacienda was in a state of long and continual decline, and Anita's clothing was patched and oversized. Dex gathered that she must have been losing weight recently else she would already have had her clothes altered to a proper fit.

He wondered how he could manage to avoid giving offense and yet—

"Now that the official purpose for my visit has been taken care of, miss, and I know my apologies will be conveyed to your grandfather, could I ask a favor of you?"

"You may ask, certainly."

"I love the sound of children having a good time. Would it be acceptable if I were to, um, sponsor a party for the children I noticed out there." He motioned in the general direction of the hacienda yard.

Anita looked puzzled by the request. "Do you mean to say a . . . fiesta?"

"Yeah. Sort of. Not for any special reason but just because it's fun. And I wouldn't have to be there myself, you see. I'll be leaving as soon as my clothes are cleaned and ready. But I'd like to, oh, throw a party for those kids. It would please me very much. Do you think your grandfather would permit it?"

"I . . . do not know."

"Well, I tell you what. I'll assume that it's all right with him and make it possible, all right? Would you mind?"

"I suppose . . . that is, I think—"

"Thanks," he said quickly, before she could put any roadblocks in his path. He had, he thought, fifty-some dollars loose in his trousers pocket and of course more tucked away in the money belt. He would leave the fifty, he thought. That should help fill the larder for a while.

He had another swallow of the lemonade. The taste was growing on him. But now he felt a little guilty for having taken the lemons and honey away from the people who lived here in order to provide for a guest.

The sense of guilt lasted only for a moment though when he thought of his own family and how a similar situation would have been dealt with by his father or his grandfather. Hospitality and good manners would most assuredly have taken precedence with either of them, just as it now did with Don Cesar Whatever Whatever Whatever Espinoza and his clan. In fact it would have been insulting if he refused their sacrifice. He lifted his glass in a salute to Don Cesar's lovely granddaughter and drank deep of the lemonade.

• 12 •

Perhaps someone in the household was eavesdropping and conveying information to the others. Or, hell, for all Dex knew these New Mexicans had some sort of mystic powers that enabled them to know the thoughts of others. For whatever reason, though, by the time he excused himself for the four hour ride back to town, the whole hacienda community of family and hands seemed to regard him as a benefactor.

The children who'd been hiding and peeping were now swarming around his legs like an oversized litter of friendly puppies. They laughed and touched and clamored for his attention until he felt like a politician on the day after election. The winning politician, that is.

Dex wished he had some candies or something to distribute to them, but they had to settle for pats and gentle pinches instead.

Anita, accompanied by the harpy with the broom, eventually shooed them away and Dex's horse was brought around by the same boy who'd taken him . . . or perhaps by another who looked like him. Dex didn't bother to try and decide.

"You are a good man, Señor Yancey," Anita said as he mounted.

Dex felt a small flush of heat into his temples and hoped like hell that he wasn't blushing. "Just enjoying myself," he said.

Anita had the fifty dollars tucked somewhere on her person. He'd expected something of an argument to get her to take it, but apparently the girl had a practical nature. He'd no sooner offered it than it disappeared from his hand and into hers.

"*V'ya con Dios*," she said.

"That means good-bye in Spanish?"

She smiled up at him and shook her head as she stood beside his stirrup. "Not really."

When Anita offered no further translation Dex shrugged and reined the horse toward the sagging gate. Loudly, happy children scattered like a covey of Louisiana timberland quail, and Dex—he was feeling a mite full of himself and in a mood to show off—put his horse into a lope. As he passed through the gate he lifted his hat in salute. And considered himself damned lucky that the horse didn't spook and ruin such a fine exit.

Once he was clear of the hacienda, though, he pulled the bay to a walk and then had to fiddle with it for a bit to get it to take a distance-eating extended walk. It was a long way back to Huaca Guadalupe, and they hadn't offered him a meal at the Espinoza hacienda.

Oh shit, Dex thought as he reached the top of the knoll he'd crossed earlier and found himself facing three rather rough-looking men. The three were mounted and spread unnaturally far apart, one squarely in the middle of the road and the other two flanking him from a distance of a good eight or ten yards.

Highwaymen, Dex thought immediately.

His second immediate thought was of the money belt around his middle. Where the hell was James when Dex needed him, dammit?

The bay horse slowed without Dex's conscious volition and came to a stop when the man in the roadway turned his horse sideways to block Dex's passage.

"Something I can do for you gents?" Dex asked with an easy manner and a charm-the-nuts-off-a-snake sort of smile. The words and the smile were only a facade to buy time while he tried to work out a sequence of motion.

The closest was this one immediately before him. He would have to shoot that one first. Then snap a shot at the man to his left. Then—if he was still alive and functioning—he would try to swing all the way around to his right for a shot at that one. Maybe roll out of his saddle first since his back would be exposed to that third man as soon as he turned to get the second.

Damned small chance for all of that to work out, of course. Not with the odds being what they were. But he couldn't think of anything better if confrontation turned into gunfire.

"You're white," the middle man, who seemed to be the leader of this small pack, said to him.

Dex nodded. "Yes, I've been white for quite a long time now. Why would that surprise you?"

The man said something in a halting and awkward Spanish so bad that even Dex could tell he was mangling the language, then nodded in the direction of the Espinoza hacienda.

"Sorry, but I didn't catch a word of that."

"You don't talk that lingo?"

Dex shook his head. "Never heard it back home. One hears quite a lot of French. And of course Latin and Greek at school. Then there is the Creole patois, but that's mostly in the bayous. No Spanish though. Sorry."

The man looked confused by that. Dex didn't mind.

Dex used the heel of his left foot, which was out of sight from where these men sat, to bump his horse's belly while holding his rein tight. The horse, confused, naturally became fidgety and began to toss its head. Dex quit prodding with his foot and leaned forward to stroke the bay's neck and calm the nervousness he himself had induced.

While he was doing that he took a moment to assess the opposition. The man directly in front of him appeared to be the most dangerous of the three. All of them were armed with large revolvers—it seemed the men in this western country all favored guns large enough to bludgeon boar hogs with and never mind the concept of small but accurate—and one of them had a long arm of some sort stuffed into a canvas sack that dangled from his saddle horn. The good news was that none of them had their firearms in hand. Yet.

Their leader was clean shaven and of medium build. The other two were both very large men who had the look of the empty-headed bullies about them. All wore the rough and durable clothing of the ranch hand in this country, heavy trousers, long sleeved shirts buttoned to the throat, vests, hats with huge brims, gaudy neckerchiefs, and gauntlet-style gloves with fancy embroidering or beadwork on the leather cuffs.

It occurred to Dex that the gloves being still in place was probably a very good sign. One way or another, gloves would make a man slower and slightly more awkward if he had to go for his gun in a hurry. And the fact that they were still wearing them rather than tucking them behind their belts probably meant that their initial intent was not to shoot. Dex rather liked that notion.

"Where you from, mister?"

Dex told him.

"That's not around here," the fellow said, stating the obvious.

"No, it isn't."

"What're you doing messing with those stinking greasers then?"

"It was what you might consider a social call." Dex doubted any of the three of them would fully understand that. But then it wasn't his place to educate them.

The man on the left, a burly fellow with a reddish tinge in his full beard, edged closer and said, "This's the fella that was showin' Selma off at breakfast th'other day, Ben."

"Say is that right, mister?" the one called Ben asked, his interest obviously piqued. "You had you some of that purty little greaser gal? She a good fuck, is she?"

"A gentleman never kisses and tells," Dex told him.

All three of the men got something of a kick out of that. Their humor seemed considerably lighter—and less menacing—afterward.

"Hell, man, I can't blame you for makin' your social call if you got to stick it in little ol' Selma again. She's a snooty little bitch, but she's mighty purty. I got to say that, greaser or no, that Selma she's purty."

"She is pretty, indeed," Dex agreed.

"Listen, mister, we didn' mean to cause you no trouble. Just kinda wonderin' what a white man would want with those stinking spics. You know?"

Dex didn't know actually. Didn't want to either. He admired and rather liked old Don Cesar, in fact. From the one brief glimpse of the old man's character that Dex had, Don Cesar reminded him quite a lot of his own proud Southern family.

Greasers? Stinking spics? Dex didn't think so.

On the other hand, it was not a point that he particularly wanted to debate with these . . . um . . . gentlemen.

At least not out here in the road when there were three of them and only one of him.

Another time, perhaps.

"If you gentlemen would excuse me, it's a long way back to town, and I'm rather hungry."

"Sure thing, mister. Didn' mean t'trouble you none."

Ben backed his horse out of Dex's way, and the other two allowed their mounts to drift in closer. It was obvious there would be no gunplay and so their spread formation—it occurred to Dex that this was a practiced move on their part—was no longer necessary.

"Good day, gentlemen." Dex touched the brim of his hat in a salute that was much more mocking than heartfelt and bumped his horse into a lope again. And this time he held the gait for a considerable distance. He wanted as far away from that odd threesome as he could get.

· 13 ·

It was too late for lunch and too early for supper but Dex was hungry enough to eat the ears off his horse so he stopped at the café without even bothering to take the animal—with or without its ears attached—back to the livery.

Between Dex's gestures and Pancho's vacant smiles a meal was ordered and quickly delivered.

Dex was beginning to worry. He was beginning to actually like this Mexican cooking. Surely that was a sign of something bad, although he couldn't for the life of him figure out exactly what. In any event he dug deep into the tortillas, chunks of peppered meat—goat, he thought—drenched in gravy, seasoned rice, and a huge helping of a reddish brown mess that had something of the consistency of mashed potatoes but tasted like . . . he wasn't entirely sure what it tasted like. But he liked it, whatever it was.

He wolfed down enough food for three hungry lumberjacks, or it felt like that much anyway, and sat back with a feeling of contentment to nurse a beer and belch a little in the shade while out on the street, the life of Huaca Guadalupe passed by.

Dex considered that a valid observation despite the fact that the main street of the town was for the most part empty. A pair of untended burros wandered along the sidewalk, stopping frequently to nibble at the tops of weeds growing out through the boards. Half a block from them a brown and white dog came out of one alley, sniffed its way past the front of a hardware store and disappeared back into the next between-building alley opening.

Huaca Guadalupe was as quiet as—

Dex came to his feet with a rush as he heard a woman's scream nearby. Shriek was more like it. Whoever it was and whatever the cause, she sounded damned frightened.

It could be nothing more than some señora who was being disciplined by her husband.

But it sounded more serious than that.

Dex was done eating anyway. And that first scream was followed quickly by another.

Without waiting for Pancho to figure out how much Dex's meal cost, he tossed a half dollar down and left the rest of his beer behind so he could stretch his legs and hustle down the street toward the edge of town.

The woman screamed again and now Dex was close enough to hear a sound that he remembered well from his childhood, the sound of a leather strap slapping hard on living flesh.

Dex followed the commotion around the side of the town smithy and behind it to a mud-walled corral. The noises were coming from inside the enclosure.

He located the gate and yanked it open.

Well, well, well, he silently mused. Fancy this. Apparently the boys he'd talked with on the road in from the Espinoza place had been really taken by the idea of having a crack at Anselma.

It was the three men Dex encountered earlier who were swinging a length of latigo and Selma who was doing the screaming. She was not the party who was being whipped, however. A teenaged Mexican boy—he could have been the same kid who'd taken Dex's horse out there at the hacienda but he wasn't positive about that—was held pinned against the rear wheel of one of those odd-looking wagons he'd last seen in the Espinoza yard. One of the bully-boys held the kid while the smaller Ben cut him with one vicious swipe of the leather after another. Ben looked like he was enjoying himself.

While those two were occupied with the boy, the second bearded plug-ugly had Selma wrapped up and immobile. There was no question that this one liked what he was doing. He had one small tit squeezed tight inside a powerful grip and he was kneading it like it was fresh dough yet to rise.

Selma kept screaming and Ben kept whipping and the kid at the wheel was trembling from the pain but had his teeth gritted tight and looked damned well determined that he would not, no matter what, give these sons of bitches the satisfaction of letting out so much as a whimper. If they damned well killed him they wouldn't hear him holler 'uncle' first.

None of the crowd of them noticed they were no longer alone inside the blacksmith's corral.

Dex hadn't much liked the odds of facing these three

back on the road earlier, and he didn't like those same odds any better now.

So, he concluded, the logical thing to do would be to either turn tail and move smartly along . . . or shorten the odds.

He really wasn't much in a mood at the moment for running away while a young woman who'd been nice to him got mauled and mistreated by a big ugly SOB like this one.

Dex looked around. A discarded singletree with one end broken off lay at the base of the mud wall close to the gate. Dex picked that up and weighed it in his hand. It didn't have quite the heft or balance of a properly turned base ball bat. But its hickory was just as tough.

Dex stepped quietly behind the man who was groping Selma, took a comfortable stance . . . and whaled the be-jabbers out of the big SOB.

From behind. Without warning. Hard.

The blow was unfair. No question about it. And Dex probably should have felt damned well ashamed of himself.

He didn't.

The singletree hit the back of the man's head with a sound like a melon being thumped, and the fellow dropped dead away taking Selma down to the ground with him.

Selma shrieked again.

Neither of the other two paid the least attention to that, of course. Selma had been screaming her lungs out for some minutes now and no one seemed to so much as notice it.

With a shrug, Dex took a fresh grip on his trusty singletree and went stalking another scalp for his trophy belt.

He almost got it done. Almost. When he was within three or four paces of Ben, the piece of dumb muscle who was holding the kid noticed Dex's presence—he'd been in plain view for a good couple minutes so it was about time, really—and signified the arrival of company by rolling his eyes wildly and croaking a sound that may well have been intended as a warning, although he did not manage any coherent form of speech.

Ben got the message. He whirled, leather strap raised ready to strike. Dex would've bet his last dollar on the idea that good old Ben was expecting to see Selma coming at his backside. The man was not prepared to face a grown man instead.

"Surprise," Dex said.

And smashed Ben over the head with the singletree.

The crown of Ben's big hat probably cushioned some of the blow—dammit—but there was enough force left to send Ben's eyes rolling completely out of sight while his knees turned to water and he toppled face down into a scattering of horse apples.

It would have been nigh perfect, Dex thought, if the horse turds were only a little fresher. As it was, well, half wet would just have to do.

Dex winked at the last of the trio, who by then had let go of the Mexican boy and looked like he was trying to work out what he should do next.

Dex took pity on the big man and solved this dilemma for him by taking the several necessary steps forward and whacking this one too over the noggin.

The third fellow joined his companions in the bliss of sweet slumber and dropped like a sack of potatoes. Or, considering the local penchant for tortillas, perhaps like a sack of coarse-ground cornmeal.

Selma dashed forward to grab the arm of the boy. Both of them were sputtering and steaming like the fuses on a pair of Fourth of July Chinese crackers, and Dex would've bet that their language would blister the paint off their wagon. If there'd been any paint remaining on the weathered old piece of rolling trash.

After a moment Selma took a wild-eyed look at Ben, who was groaning and beginning to move just a little. She seemed to realize that these three were going to come around again bye and bye. And she quite obviously did not intend to be present when that event occurred.

She said something to the boy, who in turn looked at Dex and said something in Spanish that was no more comprehensible to him than Selma's words had been. The boy tried again. And then a third time. When that didn't work he shrugged and smiled and made a follow-me motion. Dex had no difficulty understanding that.

Dex wasn't as concerned as these two obviously were about making tracks before the bullies woke up.

But then he didn't have to live here in the aftermath of whatever this was all about either.

He accepted the kid's invitation and climbed inside the funny-looking box that was built onto the bed of the wagon. The inside of the wagon, rather oddly Dex thought, was fitted out like a tiny house, complete with a narrow bunk, drawers and lockers and even a miniature stove. He'd never seen anything like it and had no idea why anyone would want to make such a thing. But there it was.

Selma got inside with him, and the kid took up the driving lines and drove the rig out through the gate Dex had so thoughtfully left open. And never mind that he'd simply forgotten it while his attention was diverted.

• 14 •

Their trip wasn't a long one. The boy drove a couple blocks away and through a narrow alley to the back of one of the many adobe buildings in the town, each one of which seemed perfectly interchangeable with all the others so far as Dex could determine.

This one turned out to be a mercantile. The interior had that musty, dusty, slightly spicy scent common to general stores everywhere. Its shelves were piled heavy with jumbled bags, boxes, and cans. Hams and slabs of smoked bacon and strings of cased sausages hung from the rafters while red and black and purple strings of dried peppers were hanging along the walls, looking as much like decorations as foodstuffs.

The Mexican proprietor seemed to know where every need could be met, however, and the youngster—still limping and in obvious pain after the beating he'd just received—hurried to grab the things Selma read off a shopping list. Selma ordered, the proprietor located, and the young boy toted it all outside and into the wagon. Where he found room to put it all Dex didn't know, but everything disappeared inside.

What they were loading, of course, was food. It was obvious that Selma and the kid had come to town so they could lay in supplies with the "party" money Dex gave them. Which was his intention when he suggested the ruse.

The purchases, he noticed, were long on bulk and low of price. Cornmeal and rice were the basics along with huge sacks of dried beans—Dex could hardly believe a skinny teenager could carry the bulky sacks without assistance, and while he was already in pain at that—a little sugar, a little salt, and pail after pail of lard.

They bought no meat at all. Too expensive, he guessed. He tried to remember if there had been chickens or hogs at the rancheria but if there were, he couldn't remember seeing them. Not that it was any of his business. But, dammit, growing children need meat in their bellies, too.

Dex forced back an impulse to add things to the list Selma was carrying. It wasn't any of his damned business.

When the loading was done and something—he didn't have any difficulty figuring out what—passed from Selma's hand into that of the proprietor, Dex followed the two outside to the wagon.

He only intended to say good-bye so they could get on their way back to the hacienda.

That idea was laid aside when he saw Selma's eyes widen in fear as she stepped out the back door of the mercantile.

Dex followed her gaze. Ben and company were there. Mounted. Blocking the mouth of the alley where the wagon was parked. There was no way the Espinozas' pair of skinny mules could muscle the wagon backward the entire length of the alley, so in order for Selma and the boy to leave they would necessarily have to pass the bullies who were unfortunately awake and aware now. Dammit.

Things would have been much more comfortable if these three had only stayed unconscious lying there in the dirt and the horse crap of that corral for another hour or so.

Dex's first thought was to regret that he'd left the second Webley tucked away in his saddlebags back at the hotel. Even his sword was there in his room. All he had with him at the moment were six shots in the one revolver he was carrying.

Three men. Six cartridges. What the hell. That would just have to be enough. He did *not* intend to allow a repeat of the earlier abuse, especially since he had the idea that these three were only beginning to enjoy themselves so far as Selma was concerned. He suspected she'd have been raped half a dozen times by now if he hadn't come along and the abuse still going on. God knew what would have happened to the boy as well.

Selma was much too nice a girl to allow something like that to happen, damn them. The men were not going to get a second chance.

Dex motioned Selma and the kid into the back of the wagon, then climbed into the driving box himself and took up the lines.

If these boys wanted a fight they could damned well have one.

The men were only thirty or forty feet away and could see him clearly. Dex nodded and grinned at them, then touched the butt of his stubby .455 to let them know what their choices were. If they wanted to get that serious about it, they were welcome.

With a sharp cluck of the tongue Dex took a light contact with the mules' bits and shook the line to ease them forward into their harness.

The now heavy wagon creaked and groaned and the iron tires crunched over gravel and hard-baked earth as they began to roll forward.

· 15 ·

Apparently none of these boys wanted to die today. Dex could see Ben's lips move as the leader of the trio said something to his companions, then Big and Bigger—as Dex had begun thinking of them—wheeled their horses and moved out of the way.

Ben lingered a few moments longer, then nodded very solemnly in Dex's direction and backed his grulla out of the alley mouth in as pretty a move as a body could want to see. Fine animal, that one. Nice neck on it.

It occurred to Dex—although he'd have been happier if he hadn't thought about it—that when he came out of the alley he would be between Ben on the one side and Big and Bigger on the other. No matter which direction he looked, someone would be off the other way.

Still, barring the sudden development of eyes on the sides of his head like a horse has, he would just have to make out the best he could. And he figured the best of this possibly bad situation would be for him to pay attention to Ben and not the pair of plug-uglies. Ben hadn't had time to lay out any elaborate plan for his dull minions and Dex doubted either one of them would have gumption enough to start anything on his own. Ben was the one Dex intended to keep an eye on.

The mules exited the alley into the street and Dex on the driving box of the strange little wagon a couple moments behind them.

Ben was sitting close by, his horse standing with its ears forward and head high. Dex did like that animal. Seemed a shame such a nice horse belonged to such a shitty human being.

No one drew a gun—Dex included—nor so much as moved until the wagon was well out into the street and turning toward the edge of town.

"You can't nursemaid those stinking greasers forever, boy," he heard Ben grumble as he passed by the man and rolled on.

Which was, of course, the natural truth.

Selma's wagon was heavy, now laden with its load of foodstuffs for those kids and all the others at the hacienda. And even if it hadn't been a couple spavined and scrawny old mules, they weren't going to outrun Ben and company if they decided to follow and take another crack at Selma and the boy once they were clear of town.

There was only one person in town Dex knew who could speak both Spanish and English and who he could be reasonably sure would be willing to help Selma. Dex decided to find him.

He drove the wagon to Pancho's cafe and stopped outside the arbor, sitting there and shouting Pancho's name in as loud and annoying a tone as he could manage until the fat Mexican came out, if not to help then at least to make the disturbance go away.

"Si, señor?" he asked and quite a lot more, none of which Dex came close to understanding.

"Señor Clay," Dex said.

Pancho returned something that was fast and incomprehensible.

"Señor Clay," Dex said. "Señor Clay." And kept repeating it over and over, his voice overriding Pancho's, until finally the restaurateur gave in and pointed.

Dex shook his head and motioned for Pancho to join him on the driving box of the wagon. The Mexican did so, if reluctantly, and Dex wheeled the wagon into a wide turn back into town.

Ben, Big, and Bigger were lurking on horseback a block down the street. Dex couldn't help but notice that Pancho crossed himself and mumbled something—it didn't sound like a prayer, but then what the hell did Dex know when it came to praying in Spanish—when they passed the three uglies.

When they were almost to the middle of town, Pancho grabbed Dex by the elbow and pointed again, this time at the bank building.

"Clay's the town banker?" Dex asked.

Pancho only shrugged and pointed again.

"Okay, thanks." Dex parked the wagon and thought about going inside the bank, then glanced back toward Ben and Bigger. There was no sign now of Big. "You go get him," Dex said, giving Pancho a nudge toward the bank building and resuming his monotonous litany of "Señor Clay, Señor Clay" until Pancho got the idea and went not inside the adobe-walled bank building but around toward the back of it.

The back door of the wagon popped open and Selma stuck her head out, then promptly disappeared when from a block away Big hooted loudly and made an exceedingly vulgar gesture.

Dex glared at the son of a bitch. But you can't go around shooting people off their horses just for being lewd. Unfortunately.

He sighed and turned his attention back to the place where he'd last seen Pancho.

• 16 •

"**P**ancho thinks you are a very strange man, Mr. Yancey," Clay said after conversing briefly with the restaurateur and seeing him off toward the café.

Ambrose Clay had been buttoning his shirt collar and straightening his tie when he came outside, obviously interrupted while relaxing, but now he looked like he'd never been mussed or hurried in his life. As Dex recalled the man had looked very much that same way the other day after besting Dexter in their informal bout of fisticuffs.

"Nothing strange about me," Dex returned.

Clay smiled. "Oh, I don't know. Pancho does have a point. If nothing else, I don't believe I've ever before seen a white man driving a sheepherder's caravan."

"Is that what this thing is?"

"Yes. A caravan or a sheep wagon if you prefer. The sheepherders live in them. They are fitted out as mobile accommodation. Or so I'm told. I've never actually seen inside one."

"Then this is your opportunity," Dex said. "I have a couple very frightened young people in the back of this one. They don't speak English and I don't speak Spanish, and I'd like to ask your help so I can figure out how to keep them from being assaulted again this afternoon."

"Again, you say?"

Dex explained.

"Then by all means, Mr. Yancey, let me talk with them for you."

The two Anglos left the mules tied to a post outside the Huaca Guadalupe bank and climbed onto the back steps of the sheep wagon. They would have gone inside except there was not enough room for four, not after fifty dollars' worth of bulk food supplies had already been loaded into the little rig.

Ambrose Clay and Selma had a long and heated—or so it sounded to Dex—exchange, followed by another less exhaustive conversation with the boy, whose name turned out to be Paco.

"I am surprised anyone would have done such a thing," Clay said eventually. "At the very least I'm surprised they would have attempted it here in town."

"Which is what I'm worrying about now," Dex admitted. He looked down the street, but now Ben and both the uglies were out of sight. "The one called Ben as good as told me they would wait along the road and finish what they started when I'm not around to protect these two. How'd they get this far without being caught anyway?" he asked. "Those three were blocking the road when I left the Espinoza place."

"They said they saw the men talking to you on the hill so they took the wagon and sneaked around to the south and swung wide. They don't know how the men knew they got past. They wanted to hide the sheep wagon inside the corral so no one would see them, but the men found them there." Clay shrugged. "My guess is that Turlock or one of his people saw the dust from their wheels and guessed someone slipped by."

"Turlock?" Dex asked.

"Ben Turlock," Clay said. "From your description I'd say his companions are Arthur Broyle and Ev Gardner."

"I've been calling them Big and Bigger."

Clay laughed. "That certainly fits. Anselma says you took all three on and personally beat them in a fistfight?" Clay wore a highly skeptical expression when he repeated that.

"Good Lord, no." Dex told him what happened.

"Not sporting," Clay commented. "But practical. Eminently practical."

"Yes, but that was then. This is now. I expect I'm going to have to ride all the way back out there with this wagon to make sure those kids have food to eat come breakfast tomorrow."

"Would you like company on your journey?" Clay offered.

"That's damned nice of you, Mr. Clay."

"I'd be happy to accompany you." The handsome young gent smiled. "But only if you'll start calling me Brose. All my friends do."

"If you will honor me by calling me Dex."

The two shook hands, and Brose Clay offered a fairly lengthy explanation in Spanish to Selma and Paco.

"Paco can drive the wagon," Dex suggested. "We'll

swing by the livery to pick up my horse. What about you, Brose?"

"Oh, I don't own a mount. Too much of a nuisance," he said. "Damn things eat whether they're needed or not, I discovered. And I'm not all that fond of riding anyway. I prefer to hire a rig and drive if I need to travel outside the town limits. May I make a suggestion?"

"Of course."

"Why don't you ride in the wagon with the youngsters. That way nothing can separate the wagon from both protectors at once. If the buggy broke a wheel, for instance. Then when we reach the hacienda and everyone is safe, you can ride back to town with me." Brose smiled. "It will give us a chance to become better acquainted, and I think I would like that."

"That sounds agreeable to me," Dex told him.

Clay offered more explanations in Spanish, then he and Dex dropped to the ground and followed the wagon on foot while Paco drove to the livery.

Within twenty minutes their two-wagon train pulled out on the way to the Espinoza hacienda, Paco driving the sheep wagon with Dexter and Selma inside while Brose Clay followed close behind in a hired rig.

· 17 ·

No wonder Selma and Paco hadn't made room for them inside the sheep wagon. The only space that wasn't piled ceiling high with boxes, bags, and bundles was the bunk— which Dex guessed wasn't built strong enough to hold that much weight or it would have been stacked too—and about a one foot–wide gap at the very back of the wagon next to the door.

In order for the two of them to have any measure of comfort at all, Selma had to sit cross-legged on the foot end of the bunk while Dex braced himself against the door.

And that proved to be a poor idea once they began moving. The flimsy door latch came open and Dex very nearly tumbled out onto the ground into the trotting hoofs of Brose Clay's light buggy trailing the sheep wagon by only a few yards, close enough to avoid the boil of dust that streamed into the air behind the wagon wheels.

Dex probably would have fallen if Selma hadn't

grabbed for his wrist when the door popped open. As it was Dex gave Clay a wave and Selma a rather grateful look before he squeezed himself back inside the sheep wagon and pulled the door closed again, this time making very sure that the latch was fully engaged.

Selma said something to him, which he could not understand, and then motioned, which he could.

She scooted forward toward the head of the bunk to make room for Dex to join her there.

The bunk was narrow.

And the girl was pretty.

And Dex's reaction to a combination of pretty girl and swaying bed was very soon entirely obvious.

He grinned at Selma and shrugged.

Her response was a laugh and a wink. She wriggled closer to him and reached out to touch the protrusion that quite completely destroyed the correct lie of his trousers. Dex's tailor would have been scandalized. Fortunately Selma was not. But then it wasn't like she was a timid virgin. The other night, commercial aspects aside, she'd seemed to enjoy things every bit as much as Dexter did.

"We do have time enough, don't we," Dex said. Not that Selma would understand him any better than he could comprehend her Spanish.

From there on, however, words were unnecessary. A touch here. A stroke there. One kiss led to more. Touching led to tasting.

There was ample room on the tiny bunk, it turned out, for two people to push aside the bits of clothing that were in the way and to make the single beast that has two backs.

Dex burrowed deep inside the sweet girl's flesh and held himself there, letting the rocking, jolting movement of the sheep wagon do the work—and pleasurable work it was—within.

He could feel Selma's breathing quicken and become ragged as the arrhythmic motion teased her into arousal and beyond. After several exquisitely enjoyable minutes of that odd sensation, Selma gasped and clutched frantically at him, clinging to him with her arms and legs alike as spasms of pleasure washed through her slim body.

She clamped her teeth tight shut but the explosion of her climax must have been too much to contain. Or for all he knew, maybe the girl just didn't give a damn.

In the final throes of release she cried out aloud.

From only a foot or two away on the opposite side of a very thin wood and canvas partition Paco said something.

Selma giggled and answered him. This time Dex rather wished he knew what the girl was saying.

Not that he was interested in dwelling on questions of language. Not at that exact moment he was not because he could feel his own sap begin its insistent, demanding climb from his balls as the pressure rose beyond his ability to contain or so much as delay.

Warm, liquid joy spewed from his body into hers as Dex filled Selma with the essence of life and pleasure.

He wanted to cry out too in testament to the power of his release, and it was all he could do to clamp his jaw shut and keep the shouts of triumph inside.

After all, what could he say to Paco to explain away the perfectly obvious?

Dex smiled down into Selma's pretty face and kissed the girl as the movement of the wagon continued to slide his no longer insistent cock in and out, back and forth.

And soon, delightfully soon, the bumping, sometimes

jarring motion began to weave a new, more relaxed spell of pleasure.

Dex laughed at the look of joy in Selma's eyes when she felt the change taking place inside her body. She laughed and hugged him close and began once again to respond with her own quick arousal.

Funny thing, Dex thought, but just a little while ago he'd been grumbling to himself about how long the trip out to the hacienda would take.

Now he only wished they had further to drive.

• 18 •

Brose pulled the buggy horse to a stop at the top of the knoll east of the hacienda. Dex thought it an odd place to stop again since the horse shouldn't need rest already. It had been standing still for half an hour or so down at the Espinoza place while Selma and Paco delivered impassioned comments about their treatment in town and the rest of the family tried to express their gratitude to Dex and Brose for helping the youngsters out of the jam.

Now, though, Brose was stopping again for some reason. Dex rather wished he would hurry on. It was already hours past nightfall and they still had a long way to drive before they could get back to town for a beverage and a bite—they'd been invited to eat at the rancheria, but Dex hadn't wanted to use up any of the clan's meager supply of foodstuffs. In fact he was already thinking about talking with the mercantile owner about an arrangement that would keep food in those kids' bellies.

"What's up?" Dex asked when Clay wrapped the driving lines around the whip socket as if he intended to sit there for a while.

"You'll see in a mo—never mind, here we are."

Dex did see as seconds later three forms on horseback materialized out of the darkness.

It was, by damn, Ben and his bullyboys, back on duty atop the knoll overlooking the hacienda. They'd not been seen during the drive out from town. Now they were back.

The three rode closer and Dex half-consciously reached down to touch the butt of his Webley for reassurance.

Big and Bigger—Brose had mentioned their names earlier, but Dex had no idea which was which; and besides, he liked his version better anyway—stopped several yards away but Ben rode close to the buggy and stopped there, removing his hat deferentially.

"I'm sorry, Mr. Clay sir. I hope we did the right thing, seeing as you was riding along with the spics this evening."

"You did exactly right, Ben. I knew I could count on you. Good man."

Dex was—flabbergasted was too mild a term for it.

Just what the fuck was going on here anyway?

Brose turned to Dex and said, "Dexter, my friend, I'd like you to meet these gentlemen." He performed the introductions quickly. Big turned out to be Ev Gardner while Bigger was Arthur Broyle. By any name Dex didn't like the sons of bitches. Nor their leader Turlock for that matter. But what was—

"The gentlemen," Clay was saying, although certainly he knew as well as Dex did that these three were as far from being gentlemen as pigs are from being race horses, "work for me."

It was a good thing Dex wasn't in the middle of swallowing anything at the time. He would have spit it all over himself.

"They—"

Clay laughed and nodded. "That's right. They do. Or more accurately they are employed by a gentleman whom I represent." Clay turned back to Turlock and said, "You are doing a fine job out here, Ben. Just keep it up if you please."

"Thank you, Mr. Clay. We were kinda worried . . . you know . . . about letting the greasers by. But with you being right there and everything, well, we thought—"

"You did just right." Clay lifted an admonishing finger. "But no more shenanigans in town, Ben. Let's keep it out here where there aren't witnesses, all right?"

"Yes sir, Mr. Clay. It's just that that girl," Ben chuckled, "that's one ripe little senorita if you know what I mean, sir."

"Yes, she is, but there are limits. Keep that in mind, will you. Not in town." Clay laughed. "Now if you can get her on the ground out here, you boys go ahead and enjoy yourselves. In fact, if you get hold of her out here, save some for me, you hear?"

Ben and Big and Bigger joined into the laughter then. Oh, that was a fun thought, wasn't it.

Funny. Dex didn't much feel like participating.

"You can go on back to what you were doing, boys," Clay said as he unwrapped the lines from the whip socket and sorted them through his fingers. "Just keep up the good work."

"Yes sir, Mr. Clay. Thank you, sir."

Brose put the buggy into motion, wheeling quickly away from the bullyboys, who were quickly lost to sight in the darkness. When they'd gone about a quarter mile in silence—Clay for whatever reasons of his own and Dex because he was just plain speechless—Brose turned and said, "If you don't have dinner plans tomorrow, Dexter, there is a gentleman I'd like you to meet. I've been thinking while we drove out here and all the more so since I saw your reception back there at the hacienda. I believe there could be a place for you in Sir David's plans."

"Sir, you said?"

"That's right. The real thing. An English gentleman. Quite distinguished as you shall see for yourself soon enough if you're interested. Would mid-day tomorrow be convenient for you?"

"I, uh . . . mid-day tomorrow would be just fine, thank you."

"Then with your permission I'll call for you at the hotel about eleven. Is that acceptable?"

"Yes. Fine."

Dex's thoughts were running fast and furious right now—literally and liberally laced with fury, in fact—but one thing he already knew for certain: If Brose Clay wanted to offer Dex a "place" in whatever this ugliness was about, why, Dex wanted to hear every detail and nuance. And what better way to learn than straight from the mouth of this British nobleman Sir David Piece-of-Shit or whothefuckever.

⋄ 19 ⋄

Clay hadn't said but Dex assumed they would set out from the hotel and walk to wherever it was in Huaca Guadalupe this Sir David person lived. Or worked. Or whatever it was he did so far away from Merry Aulde England. Instead Clay showed up driving the same hired buggy as before, although this time with a different horse between the poles.

"Good morning, friend Dexter. You look bright of eye today."

"Good morning yourself," Dex returned. Today he really didn't feel like calling Ambrose Clay 'friend'.

"Ready?"

"And raring," Dex told him. That much was certainly true. His curiosity had only grown overnight, and he was eager to meet this Britisher and hear what the man had to say.

It must be something almighty . . . interesting . . . to justify beating and raping innocents.

Dex climbed onto the passenger side of the buggy seat, adjusted the set of his hat, and motioned Clay forward. Clay clucked to the horse and shook the lines a bit and the piebald gelding stepped out into a lively road pace.

"Going far?" Dex asked.

"A fair distance," Clay said without further explanation.

Dex shrugged and settled back into the padded glove leather upholstery. He figured he might as well make himself comfortable as long as he was going to be here.

"Nice," Dex said as they came around a bend and through a copse of large trees to break into the open again with an impressively large house and outbuildings before them.

Except for a few sheds and barns and other constructions of little importance this was about the only wooden frame structure Dex could recall seeing in this part of New Mexico Territory.

Sir Fuckyouverymuch seemed not to be worrying about when the next remittance check would arrive from the folks back home. It was obvious that a considerable outlay of cash would've been required to put together so grand a spread as this one. And the construction was all new. The gateposts they drove between had not yet had time to weather into gray, and the white-painted trim on the three story brown house was still bright and spanking fresh. The house lacked a colonnaded porch but otherwise would not have looked out of place on a Louisiana plantation.

The outbuildings would have all seemed normal enough in that context, too, except here there were no storehouses for the bales of cotton. Instead there were sets of chutes and small fenced enclosures covering, Dex guessed, the better part of five acres, maybe more.

The only animals so far visible around the place were horses, mostly light saddle stock, but for the past half hour they'd been passing bunches of grazing cattle, a dozen here, half a dozen there.

"This is a beef-producing ranch, right?" Dex asked.

Clay nodded. "A good many of Sir David's friends have become fabulously wealthy in the beef business up north. They also tell him, though, about heavy winter losses. That's why Sir David is putting his operation together down here. We have mild winters here and very strong grass. Not so much of it as on the northern grasslands, you understand. So the trick down here should be to allow for a much larger allotment of grazing land per cow-calf unit."

"Uh huh." The amazement was that Dex understood that. Mostly. But then it was simple logic, wasn't it.

Clay smiled. "Sir David is a real go-getter. He intends to outperform his friends in every aspect of the business."

"Uh huh," Dex said again. No tongue-tied conversationalist, he.

"Up north they report calf crops of roughly twenty percent of the heifers and cows of breeding age."

"Uh huh."

"Sir David believes he can increase that to thirty, perhaps even forty percent when he brings in blooded bulls from England and uses a controlled environment for breeding. That's what all those corrals over there are for." Clay nodded in the general direction of the pens that sprawled over so much of the land area close to the house.

"The bulls will be kept there in that long barn and brought to the cows when the cows come in season. It will be a lot of work, but Sir David believes it will pay off in a much improved calf crop."

"Uh huh."

"Well." Clay drew back on the lines and brought the rig to a halt. "Here we are."

A black kid of ten or twelve darted around the corner of the house and came to take the horse by the bit to hold it while the gentlemen climbed out of the buggy.

"Is the, um, is Sir David expecting us?" Dex asked.

"I sent a note out last night. Hungry?"

"As a bear."

"You won't be disappointed. Sir David sets a fine table."

Dex took a moment to brush the road dust from his clothes and check the knot in his tie. Then he nodded and followed Clay to the massive double doors at the entryway.

He was as ready as he was ever likely to get.

Now if he could just keep himself from throttling the old son of a bitch . . .

• 20 •

Sir David Francis Manchester was not exactly what Dex might have expected.

White hair, fluffy mustache, silk dressing gown, clipped accent, striped trousers, portly build, bulbous nose, arrogant bearing—all of those things Dex half expected and certainly would have accepted without a second thought.

None of them could be used to remotely describe the man Ambrose Clay introduced in the trophy room of the mansion.

Sir David turned out to be in his early twenties at the oldest. And could have passed for a smooth-cheeked eighteen if he wanted. He was a lean and compact five and a half feet or so with close-cropped blond hair and something of a schoolboy look about him that his delicate build and diminutive stature only served to emphasize. Dex doubted he would weigh in at much more than a hundredweight, and he probably could have had an excellent career as a jockey if that had been his inclination.

He wore denim trousers that showed the stains and abrasions of hard use, a dark blue pullover shirt and black and white houndstooth check vest that had the string and paper medallion of a cigarette tobacco pouch hanging where a watch fob might ordinarily belong. His boots were of the high heeled western style with extra fancy stitching. Tall as they were they couldn't hide Manchester's, um, shortcomings. But the attempt was made, yes it was. Dex couldn't be sure of the colors of thread that were used to decorate the boots because they were caked with dust and dried manure.

The British gent carried a pair of gloves with leather gauntlets tucked behind a wide, carved leather belt, and his headgear, which he tossed to a waiting servant as he made his entrance, was of the wide brimmed cowboy style so common in this part of the country.

"You'd be the Louisiana gentleman our mutual friend here has been tellin' me about," Manchester declared as he advanced on Dex with his right hand extended and a welcoming smile baring a set of impressively white teeth.

Clipped British accent? The man affected a drawl, obviously trying to ape the speech as well as the dress and manners of an American from the far west.

He almost pulled it off. Almost. Dex was able to keep from breaking out into laughter, fortunately. That would have been rude, after all. And a gentleman is never rude. Unintentionally, that is.

Dex shook the undersized, underaged Sir's hand, and Clay performed the necessary introductions.

"Yancey, you say. From Louisiana? You wouldn't have any blood connection with the Harrisons of Virginia, would you? I understand they are distant cousins of ours. Came over in 16-something-or-other and settled on a par-

cel called Berkeley Hundred if I have it right. Lost track
of them afterward though. I really should look them up
sometime."

"Sorry," Dex said.

That was not a lie. Exactly. But what he was sorry
about was that there could be a thread of connection, however tenuous, between himself and this English lord, because the truth was that between the Harrisons and the
Virginia Lees from whom Dex's mother descended there
was indeed a genealogical linkage, albeit not a close one.

And Manchester really did not know what became of
the Harrisons in this country? Well, Dex supposed it was
possible, of course, even though William Henry Harrison
was—briefly—president of the United States back in the
time of Dex's grandfather.

Still, Dex did not think he wanted to play the bloodline
games. That was something he did not particularly relish
even with southerners of his own station. He certainly did
not want to start it with this make-believe cowboy from
the far side of the waters.

"Are you gentlemen hungry?" Manchester asked, rubbing his hands together as if to warm or perhaps to wash
them.

"Very," Ambrose Clay assured him. "But you should
know that I've been bragging on the table you set here,
Sir David."

"Then I hope I'll not disappoint. This way if you
please, Mr. Yancey." Manchester turned and ushered Dex
before him out a set of sliding doors, through the entry
hall and on into a sumptuous dining room large enough
to accommodate at least half the population of a town like
Huaca Guadalupe.

Ambrose Clay, Dex noticed, was rather thoroughly ignored by the Britisher.

But then Ambrose Clay quite obviously had already accepted the gentleman's farthing and pledged his fealty in return. Manchester did not need to play up to him.

Clay had been quite right about one thing. Sir David Francis Manchester did indeed set a fine table. The place settings were exquisite, and the foods distributed by a succession of pickaninnies were almost as grand. Plump passenger pigeon awash in rich gravy, thick egg noodles fried in butter, a roast of rare beef served in its own blood, chilled oysters on the half shell—not as fresh as one might've hoped, but Dex had to grant the fellow points for his effort—and half a dozen other excellent dishes were available, each accompanied by a wine that was appropriate to the course.

Dex was impressed, and he enjoyed his meal immensely. After all, food has neither moral viewpoint nor political leaning, and fine is fine when it comes to dining.

They ate in relative silence, Manchester speaking up every once in a while to pontificate about cows and bulls and other nonsense about which Dex knew less than nothing.

There was, of course, no serious conversation. Not over dinner. That would come later, Dex anticipated, along with the brandy and cigars.

Dex was in no hurry.

· 21 ·

"Is the sherry to your liking, Mr. Yancey?"

"It's fine, thank you." But damn a man who serves sherry instead of brandy. He didn't say it. He did think it.

"Cigar?"

"No, thank you."

Poor Clay didn't even rate the offer of one of the pale-leafed Havanas, Dex noticed.

"Are you in a hurry to return to the big city, Mr. Yancey? Would you have a few minutes to spare?"

"I'm in no hurry," Dex assured him.

Manchester was still standing, although his guests were seated deep in the upholstery of pillow-soft leather armchairs. The Britisher took his time about trimming, warming, and lighting a cigar for himself.

Then, pointing the cigar as if it were a teacher's cane aiming at problems on a chalkboard, Manchester made a sweeping gesture that covered the room, the house, the northern half of New Mexico, or perhaps a land area majority of the North American continent. Dex wasn't entirely clear just yet what the Englishman intended.

"What do you think, Mr. Yancey?"

"Of your home? It's quite grand. Considering," Dex said.

That last part hadn't been what Sir David wanted to hear. If he'd just taken a drink he would surely have choked on it. As it was he blinked and for a moment seemed uncertain how he should regard the comment. "Considering?"

"Oh, you know," Dex said in an offhand manner. "The distance from real civilization. Lack of proper materials." Every board and brick was of the best and most expensive quality. At least every one that was in sight was of the very finest in both material and labor. Dex feigned a yawn and a wan smile. "You know," he repeated, certain that Manchester could with his own imagination fill in details of disregard that Dex would never have been able to think up and enumerate on the spur of the moment like this.

"Oh, I—" Manchester paused and quite literally shook his head abruptly from side to side. Tossing something away from the tip of his tongue, Dex supposed, before a wayward thought might find its way into speech. "I, um . . . I was about to say—"

"Yes?" Dex tried to sound eager to hear the little man speak. It wasn't easy.

"I, uh . . . I am intent, you know, on making the Victoria Cross the finest beef ranch in this or any country."

"Victoria Cross?" Dex asked.

"To honor her majesty the queen, of course. The initials *V* and *C* are used for our brand, don't you see." The fellow preened, puffing his chest out and lifting himself onto the tips of his high heeled riding boots. "The initials also stand for the military honor Victoria Cross, you know."

"Really? I didn't know," Dex said.

"I won the VC, you know."

"Really?"

"In the Crimea," Manchester said. "I was a subaltern with the Light Horse Brigade."

"Goodness," Dex enthused, his eyes wide. "The—what did you call it—the Victoria Cross? Imagine that."

"I'll not bore you with details. Besides, a gentleman shouldn't sound his own trumpet, don't you see. But it was quite the little dust-up. Six hundred of us charged after the guns. Only a handful emerged from that awful valley." Manchester turned his head away as if to hide some deep but unspoken emotion. "It was ghastly, sir. Ghastly."

"I'm sure it was, Sir David."

Actually Dex was beginning to enjoy himself now. After all, an artist's performance are worthy of genuine appreciation.

And this little business with Manchester now was . . . artistic to say the least.

One of the six hundred who charged the guns, eh? In the Crimea, huh? Did Manchester think Alfred Lord Tennyson wasn't read in this country?

For that matter, Manchester must've been quite the prodigy to have been a Light Horse subaltern in a Crimean campaign. Considering that he'd probably still been wearing diapers and dresses when that conflict ended. The fellow seemed to assume that Americans, mere Colonials, would have no knowledge of world affairs or recent history to make such a preposterous claim as that one.

Still, a man is entitled to his vanities and little self-glorifications, Dex supposed.

The question now was where all this folderol was headed next. And how did it relate to Anselma and Anita and old Don Cesar.

• 22 •

"My dear friend Mr. Clay informs me that you are favorably acquainted with the natives, Mr. Yancey." Dex gathered they were about to get down to cases, all the social obligations having been observed.

"Oh, I don't," Dex told him. "That may be stretching the fact."

"But you are, I believe, on good terms with the Espinoza clan."

"I would admit to that, yes."

"Are you aware that these rude bumpkins—most of them hardly understand a word of the language, after all—are you aware that they oppose progress in this territory?"

"No," Dex said. "No, I wasn't."

"It's true. Ask our friend Mr. Clay here. He's a lawyer, after all. He understands these things."

Dex looked at Clay and smiled. A lawyer, eh? He hadn't known that. Should have guessed it though, Clay having already proven himself to have feet of . . . mmm . . . clay, of course.

No wonder he'd been going steadily downhill in Dex's estimation after that initial good impression. After all, there's never been an honest lawyer, including that damn-yankee son of a bitch Abe Lincoln.

"Excuse me," Dex said, realizing that Manchester had been prattling right along and that Dex had missed the last several sentences of his discourse. "Woolgathering," he explained without really explaining just exactly what track his train of thought had been following.

"Yes, well, as I was saying, those heathen natives wish to obstruct progress in the territory. Progress which I, and the Victoria Cross, can foster on behalf of all the decent and law-abiding citizens of New Mexico Territory."

"Uh huh," Dex said with a sage nod of his head. Damn but he wished Manchester had something decent to replace this boring sherry. Heathens, he pondered, his thoughts rambling once again. Catholics almost certainly. As Dex had been raised also. And Manchester was referring to them as heathens? Dex wondered what the arrogant little Sir would say if Dex admitted to sharing that faith. Not that he practiced it. Hadn't in years. But still and all . . . Heathens.

"Just how is it that the Espinozas are obstructing progress, Sir David?" he inquired.

"They oppose development of the land by their betters."

"I see," Dex said. And so he did. The Espinozas somehow stood in the way of David Francis Manchester, he of Crimean glory and the Victoria Cross, who wanted only to benefit the masses with his rousing success and resounding profit.

"May I ask you something?" Dex asked.

"Yes, of course."

"You obviously envision a role for me in this," he suggested.

"True," Manchester conceded.

"We, um, Colonials tend to be rather brash as you may've noticed. We like to dispense with circumlocutions and come direct to the point of things."

"Yes, I know that."

"Then allow me, please, to ask the one eternal question."

Manchester seemed puzzled by that. He lifted an eyebrow and waited for Dex to proceed.

Dex smiled at the little man.

"What's in it for me?" he asked.

⋄ 23 ⋄

Manchester threw his head back and roared with laughter. It might have been the first genuine thing Dex saw in, of, or about him. Clay hesitated a split second to see which way the Sir was toppling, then joined into the jollity with some snorts and chuckles of his own.

"Damn me if I don't admire a man who's forthright," the little man said once he regained control of his breathing. "I like that, Mr. Yancey. 'Deed I do." Manchester wiped his eyes—he was back to playacting now; Dex could see that the man's eyes were clear and dry—and chortled a few times more.

"Yes, of course. What indeed *is* in it for you," the Brit posed. He turned to Clay—a more unusual event—and asked, "Tell the gentleman if you would, Mr. Clay. Am I generous to my friends?"

"Almost to a fault, Sir David."

"In coin of the realm only?"

"In that, certainly," Clay said, "but with unexpected

gifts and, shall we say, non-monetary perquisites as well."

"Blackamoors," Manchester cackled. "Brought a gaggle of kafirs over from the south of Africa, don't you see. Household servants, stable hands, all the usual, of course. Wenches, too. Nothing like a nigger wench to drain a man's sap and start his day. Or end it. I keep only the best, Mr. Yancey. Ask Mr. Clay. He's had the pleasure of sampling a few. Barely nubile little niggers just old enough to bleed. But then as the country boys like to say, big enough to bleed is big enough to butcher, eh? Ever had a nigger, Mr. Yancey? No, excuse me for asking. I forgot for a moment that you're a gentleman of the old South. Had niggers aplenty on your plantation, did you?"

"We were slave holders on a fairly large scale, yes," Dex answered honestly enough. He did not bother to add that that had been a good many years ago. Nor that he himself had never bedded a Negro girl. Not that he hadn't been interested in a dark-skinned girl now and then. He wouldn't have felt right about it, though, from thinking she might not have considered herself to have any choice in the matter. So in fact, no, he hadn't. He rather doubted Manchester would understand that.

As for Clay, well, Clay was a lawyer and they are constitutionally incapable of maintaining ethical or moral standards.

"Of course. Well, sir, accept my offer and I will compensate you more than passingly fair. I would offer you a salary of two hundred per month, plus a bonus of two thousand upon the successful completion of your, um, mission. And of course you will be welcome to enjoy any of my niggers. Any, that is, but my own private stock, eh?"

"Two hundred monthly plus bonus," Dex repeated.

"Exactly."

Dex smiled. "In pounds sterling, of course."

Manchester looked at him blankly for a moment. Then the little man began to laugh again.

"Well?"

Manchester slapped his knee. "Damn me, but you are a scoundrel, sir. A scoundrel, I say."

"Which I gather is what you are hoping for," Dex said.

Again Manchester burst out in peals of laughter. He pounded his thigh and thumped on the arm of his chair and stamped the floor with his boot heel until he regained his composure.

"Very well, sir. Pounds it shall be."

"Two hundred pounds. That would be, I believe, a thousand yankee dollars," Dex said.

Poor Ambrose Clay looked stricken when the exchange rate was mentioned. Dex gathered that Huaca Guadalupe's leading barrister had sold his own soul for something considerably less.

Thirty pieces of silver, perhaps?

"Now tell me, Sir David. Am I expected to kill Don Cesar in order to qualify for that bonus, and if so, what time deadline do I have for the job?"

Dex had successfully managed to fake a young woman's murder not too awfully long ago. He saw no reason why he couldn't pull the same piece of wool over Manchester's eyes now.

"Oh, nothing so obvious as that," Manchester said. "If that were all I wanted I could've had one of Mr. Clay's nastier friends do the dirty. No, Mr. Yancey, what I desire from you is something much more complicated than that. I want you to convince that old stick-in-the-mud to sign over his land grant holdings in my favor."

"I see," Dex said. He pursed his lips and tented his fingertips and peered silently into his palms for a moment while he considered this turn of events. Then he looked up. Both Manchester and Clay were staring at him. Dex smiled.

"I'll have the full cooperation of Brose and his employees, I take it?"

"As full as if I myself were issuing the instructions," Manchester promised.

Dex's smile turned into a wide grin as he rose from his chair and crossed the room to offer his hand to seal the bargain. "Done," he said.

"Done," Manchester repeated. "You have my word on it as a gentleman."

"Done and done," Dex said, quite thoroughly pleased that Manchester had chosen to put it just that way. Because after all, the little man's earlier misrepresentations about the Victoria Cross—the honor, that is, not the ranch—made it comfortably clear that Manchester was in fact no gentleman. Not in the way Dex understood the obligations of that honorable station.

Therefore any bargain struck with Manchester's gentlemanly pledge as its surety was no bargain at all.

Dex could consider himself free to make of this whatever he would.

· 24 ·

D_{ex}'s chum, buddy, pal and now co-worker Ambrose Clay was clearly pissed off. And Dex knew why. Clay obviously would have preferred to spend the night at the Victoria Cross as a guest of Sir David Francis Manchester. No doubt the lawyer wanted an opportunity to abuse some young black serving girl or boy—what did Dex know about the man's tastes, and he would believe anything of a lawyer—but was unable to do that when Dex said he wanted to drive back to town instead.

Of course they could have compromised. Dex could have borrowed a horse and ridden back on his own, but when Clay suggested that Dex expressed a fear that he might lose the way and become lost in the desert. Never mind that this was not really desert and forget the fact that the road was well enough traveled that it would have been difficult to stray from it. The truth was that Dex was feeling more than a trifle peeved with Clay and just plain wanted to ruffle the man's feathers. Something to do with

Clay having assumed that a Yancey would be as venal and unprincipled as he.

Well, it was working. The drive back to town was undertaken in a sullen silence on Clay's part while Dex, just to be perverse about it, nattered and prattled the whole distance, running on at the mouth about everything and about nothing, relating incidents from his childhood and bedroom exploits without end—all of which he made up on the spur of the moment. But any of them *could* have been true. More or less.

Eventually they came to a halt in front of the hotel where Dex climbed down to the ground with effusive thanks, concluding with, "You know, Brose, I've been thinking while we were on our way back. If I'm going to get the job done for Sir David, I can't let the Espinozas know that I have a side to take in this thing. I'd guess from the way Anselma and Paco accepted your help, the family doesn't know about your involvement either."

"That's right," Clay grudgingly conceded, uttering the first words he'd contributed to the conversation in probably a half hour or more, "I've kept that quiet, just in case."

"Right. But I don't want to take any chances. After all, Ben Turlock and his men report to you. Someone might see or hear something and make the connection. I think it would be better if you and I weren't seen to be openly friendly from now on. Just in case. What d'you think?"

"If that's what you think best. Sir David said I'm to take direction from you, after all."

Ah, Dex thought. That was rankling the man, too. It wasn't just a missed chance to fuck a pickanniny. Clay didn't like being made to play second fiddle now that Dex offered Manchester a Trojan horse inside the walls of the Espinoza hacienda.

"Right. If it's all right with you then, Brose, we'll kind of keep our distance, at least in public. If we need to get together, we'll do it in private and on the sly. Is there anyone you'd trust to carry messages?"

"Not really," Clay said. "The people around here are aware that Sir David needs Don Cesar's land—and by the way, it isn't really the land that's needed but the rights to the water; water is everything when it comes to livestock raising in this country—what was I saying? Oh, yes. The people. Most of them know what's going on. At the least they know that it will end with only one large outfit. I think most of them realize that Sir David with his money and his modern methods will prevail in the long run.

"But they're a stubborn bunch, most of them, and stuck in their ruts. The Espinozas have been in this country for several hundred years. Their land grants go back to the Spanish kings, almost back to the time of the conquistadors. People are used to them, and naturally all the Mexicans and mestizos would like to see old Don Cesar prevail.

"The thing that surprises me is that so many of the Anglos would side with the old man, too. I'd expected them to gather to their own kind and support Sir David, but a lot of them simply lack the foresight to go with the eventual winner. And Sir David will come out on top. You've seen for yourself what a dynamic man he is. There's no way an old fart like Don Cesar will be able to stand against him. Not in the long run."

"Sir David is dynamic, that's certainly true," Dex said. Dynamic. Or, um, something.

"Anyway," Clay said, "to get back to your question, I

trust my own men completely. Ben Turlock, I mean, along with Art Broyle and Ev Gardner. But beyond them . . . I think if you want to see me, you could leave a signal of some kind. Something in public that won't mean anything to anybody else. Then we could arrange to meet."

"Do you know which is my room in the hotel?" Dex asked.

Clay shook his head, so Dex pointed to the window and said, "If I want to see you I'll put that shade halfway up. Any ideas where and when we could meet after you see my signal?"

"How about inside the adobe corral behind the livery. I believe you know where that is," Clay said.

Dex nodded.

"At night, then. If I spot your signal I'll come to the corral, oh, about nine that same evening. How would that be?"

"Nine o'clock. Right," Dex agreed.

"All right then. Do you have any instructions until then?"

"Yes," Dex said. "I want you to pull Turlock and his men off that road blockade."

"I thought—"

"I know. You want to put pressure on the Espinozas. I understand that. But I'll be taking a different tack with them. I'm going to try and made them believe they should cooperate with Sir David. I'll make them see it will be in their own best interests to give Sir David what he needs."

"He's already tried to buy their rights fair and square," Clay said. "They wouldn't even hear him out. He tried many times. The old man wouldn't so much as speak with him in person, just sent others to meet with Sir David."

"I understand, but I think I can do it."

"How?" Clay asked bluntly.

Dex grinned. "Now that would be telling, wouldn't it?" Telling both of them, that is. Dex hadn't a clue how a person would go about trying to accomplish that deed. And had no interest in doing it even if he could come up with some ideas on the subject.

The fact was that he was taking sides in this, all right. With the Espinozas. He just couldn't manage much in the way of respect for anyone who would sanction rape and brutality as a means to enrichment.

So when it came to the gentleman from Aulde England—fuck 'im.

"About the roadblock—" Clay resumed.

"Take it off and keep it off. If I need Turlock and his people to do something else, I'll let you know. But I want that road open."

"I don't agree with you."

"You don't have to," Dex told him coldly. "But if it makes you feel any better, Brose, try to keep in mind that if my plan fails, the fault will be on my head."

He hoped that would give the lawyer cheer.

Well, sort of.

"Good night, Brose."

"G'night." Clay took up the lines and clucked to the buggy horse, rolling away in the direction not of the livery but back toward the Victoria Cross.

Dex grinned. He would've bet a fair percentage of his substance that Clay intended to go back out to the ranch on the pretext of reporting Dex's instructions and then finagle an invitation to spend the night with one of those pretty little South African blackamoors as Manchester preferred to call them.

Not that it was any of Dex's business.

He turned and went inside the hotel. It had been a rather full day and he was feeling weary.

Besides, he needed some time to do some serious thinking, because so far he hadn't an inkling of how he was going to undermine Manchester and help the old don.

• 25 •

Lordy, but he was missing James now. And not just because Dex wanted—wanted hell, needed—a friend he could lean on. James would've been damned useful now. He would have cozened and cajoled information out of the Manchester household help in a way no white man ever could. Having James around right now would've been like having eavesdropping rights on every conversation that took place inside that mansion. Convenient. But it wasn't to be, and that was the end of that.

Dex sighed and leaned back against the pillows at the head of his hotel room bed while he pondered the question of just how he should best go about shutting the door on Sir David Francis Manchester's ambitions.

He was still leaning on those pillows and still dressed in his one and only decent outfit, when dawn's pale light roused him from a less than perfect slumber.

He really should have stripped down and crawled under the sheet, dammit. As it was he felt dirty. He needed a bath; he needed a shave, and he needed a change of clothing.

He also needed some fresh ideas. Wishful thinking to the contrary, he hadn't dreamed any easy answers during the night.

And his back hurt, too, from the awkward posture he'd slept in.

At least he could count on the rest of the day going more smoothly. After a start like this almost anything would be an improvement.

He limped across the room and managed to stand almost fully upright by the time he reached the door, working the kinks out of his spine step by painful step. Why, it hardly even hurt to reach up and give the bell pull a couple brisk tugs. The bell boy this time wasn't more than a minute or two responding to the summons.

"Yes, sir?"

"I need a bath, son."

"You took a bath already this week, mister. I know 'cause I carried the water up for it myself."

"Yes, and now I'm going to take another one. With hot water this time, if you don't mind. And while I'm washing, you can go fetch my regular clothes back from the washerwoman . . . whatever her name is."

"Señora Rivera, mister."

"Right. That's the one."

"I'll have to pay her or she won't let go of them."

"How much?"

"They was awful dirty. I'd think she'll want fifty cents, maybe sixty."

"Here. Give her a dollar. But bring that hot water up first. I'll make it a quarter for you and the dollar for the washerwoman. How's that sound?"

The boy's eyes became large and round. He'd probably never seen a tip larger than a dime and that not often. Not in a bug wallow like Huaca Guadalupe, Dex guessed.

Of course if the kid was worldly wise he'd dicker Señora Rivera's price down to the original fifty cents and keep the rest for himself. But Dex would've been willing to bet that the boy was too honest for that. Too honest and too innocent. With luck maybe this youngster could avoid having to learn about people like Manchester and Clay and hang onto his innocence for a few years longer.

The boy flashed a huge grin and took off like a shot for the kitchen and the hot water reservoir.

Now if only a hot, soothing bath would help put some ideas into his head, Dex might feel like facing this day.

Forty five minutes later when he dried off, feeling like a new man with clean smelling fresh clothing and a ravenous hunger in his belly, he crossed the hotel room floor to tug at the window blind and raise it a careful halfway.

The first phase of his plan—okay, the only phase that he'd worked out as yet, but why quibble about mere details—was so deliciously invigorating that he thought it a terrible shame he'd have to wait until night before he could meet with Ambrose Clay and get it under way.

· 26 ·

"Now look, Brose. I'm not interested in excuses and I won't countenance any delays. Sir David said he wants you to cooperate fully, and I'm taking him at his word. I need that help and I need it right away. In time for breakfast tomorrow at the latest."

"But I can't possibly—"

"Shhh," Dex warned, placing a finger to his lips and looking fearfully around. Of course the corral was empty except for Ambrose Clay, Dex himself and a handful of very tired and harness-worn mules clustered down at the far end of the enclosure. There was no one within hearing, and even if someone was interested enough to try and overhear, that would have been impossible from the other side of the thick adobe walls.

But Dex thought the fretful caution a nice touch toward spurring Clay's own worries and resentments about the near future.

After all, Clay had exhibited some indications yesterday

that he was a jealous and worrying sort. And if a man gives you a stick—what the hell—hit him with it.

Clay dropped his voice to a whisper. "I really don't think—"

"I didn't ask for your approval," Dex said tersely. He hesitated for a moment and added, "I require your assistance, Clay. If you won't give it, say so. I'll ride out to the Victoria Cross and tell Sir David what I need. I'm sure he can supply it himself without bothering you."

"You don't have to—"

"What I 'have to' do," Dex said, sarcasm thick in his tone, "is have that in my hand first thing tomorrow morning. I suggest you find a way to accomplish the task. You can meet me at Pancho's cafe. No need for anyone to think the meeting is deliberate. We've run into each other there before. No one will have any reason to think differently this time. But I want you there . . . with an envelope prepared to hand to me under the table . . . or I'll ride out to have that word with Sir David after my meal. The choice is yours."

Dex turned and without waiting for acknowledgment or offering any good-byes strode swiftly out of the corral and back to the hotel for an early sleep.

He wasn't even tempted to stop in for a drink when he passed by a good five or six of the town's innumerable saloons. The thought of his last outing amid the big city excitements of Huaca Guadalupe still made him queasy.

Dex reached inside his coat—Señora Rivera had done a marvelous job of returning it to a condition fit for a gentleman's use—and pulled out a freshly starched and ironed handkerchief. Carefully he used a corner of the snowy white cloth to dab at a speck in his eye, then used it to cover a yawn before returning the handkerchief to his pocket.

When the hanky went inside his coat, though, so did the envelope Clay had surreptitiously passed him a few moments earlier. Dex coughed and dropped his napkin onto the half-eaten platter of tortillas and poached eggs swimming in chili verde that he'd been working on when Clay joined him for their carefully arranged accidental encounter.

Actually Dex would have preferred to stay a little longer and finish the meal. This Mexican food was beginning to appeal to him. Much to his delight and amazement.

The reason he did not was that he did not much feel like spending any more time than was necessary in the lawyer's company.

And judging from the tightness around Ambrose Clay's eyes when he gritted out his morning greetings, Clay felt very much the same way.

Well, it was a friendship Dex could lose without shedding any tears.

"Nice to run into you, Brose," Dex said for the benefit of anyone who might be listening.

"Likewise," Clay returned.

Dex smiled and ambled off down the street in the general direction of the livery stable. He whistled a gay tune and even attempted—badly—to twirl his cane as he strolled.

The envelope Clay had given him was lumpy and pleasantly heavy in his coat pocket.

· 27 ·

Well, well, well, as he lived and as he breathed, who was that over there but his good friends Big and Bigger. Dumb sons of bitches. They were skulking about through the alleys trying not to be seen. Which made them stand out like a pair of cow pies on a baker's shelf.

If they'd simply walked down the street Dex might not've thought anything about their presence apart from being pleased that Clay really had pulled them off the road guarding duty as instructed. As it was, sneaking about and making asses of themselves while being half-exposed to view here and again there, it was rather obvious what they were up to. And on Ambrose Clay's orders, naturally.

Not that Dex gave a shit. If Clay wanted to spy on him, that would be fine. Let the fellow peep and tattle. Dex would be happy to spin a yarn for Manchester if the little man wanted to ask. He already had his explanations and arguments well in order.

For that matter, and now that he thought of it, it probably would be a good idea for him to arrange to send a note to Manchester telling all. Or, all right, telling some. And at least a little bit of what he told would be truthful.

Good idea, Dex thought. He should do that the next time he had one of those pleasant little night-time get-togethers with Mr. Clay.

In the meantime though he had places to go, things to do, people to see.

He walked down to the livery, but this time instead of sneaking around to the corral, he went inside and whistled loudly to chase up the owner.

"Back again, Mr. Yancey?"

Since Dex was standing right there in front of him, it was perfectly obvious that, yes, he really was back again. No point in commenting on the inanity of the statement though. It was only a form of greeting after all. "Yes, sir, and I've brought a bigger wagon this time. I hope you have a boy to fill it for me. I don't feel like sweating at this early hour."

The storekeeper's attention was definitely piqued by the idea of a second and larger wagon to fill. The man did not actually salivate and cackle with glee, but the look in his eyes said that he wanted to. This would prove to be an unexpectedly profitable day for him.

"You just tell me what you want, Mr. Yancey, and where you're parked. I'll have your order filled and loaded for you quick as two shakes of a lamb's tail."

Dex began roaming through the cramped and musty aisles—not that there were so very many of them, but for Huaca Guadalupe, this store was as big as things got—pointing and deciding and feeling like a generous uncle on Christmas Eve. And whenever he came to two items that it was difficult to decide between, he settled the issue by taking both.

After all, it was David Manchester's money he was shopping with.

◆ 28 ◆

Children gathered like ants racing to the crumbs at a picnic. Dex could've sworn they were dropping out of trees. Well, except for the fact that there weren't any trees inside the compound at the Espinoza hacienda. Seemed like it anyway. Dex didn't know very much about Mexicans, but one thing he was sure of: They damn sure were breeders.

There were also some grownups in evidence this trip. Men and women of varying ages who'd stayed out of sight throughout his first visit. He hadn't honestly realized how many adults must live at the hacienda, but when he thought about it, it certainly made sense enough. There had to be adults in order to produce all these grinning, chattering, excited children.

Dex brought the big, slow freight wagon to a groaning halt, and a bunch of teenage boys came rushing out to take care of the mules for him.

His arrival hadn't been expected, but obviously he was

accepted as a welcome guest here and not as a suspicious stranger this trip. He only wished he had some Spanish to tease the kids in. Both he and the children managed to make do with mime and exaggerated facial expressions.

Another thing he was able to get across without words was that the young men should unload the wagon and put the supplies away. Dex no sooner climbed down from the driving box than the mules were led around toward the back of the hacienda, presumably to a communal storehouse, for disposition of the goodies.

Dex hadn't had time to reach the verandah before Anita came out to meet him. No scrawny witch with a broom this time but the spokeswoman herself. Dex felt honored. Sort of.

"Greetings. And *gracias. Muy gracias.*"

Dex raised an eyebrow.

Anita smiled. "It means 'thank you, thank you very much'."

Dex removed his hat and swept it before him as he bowed to the lady. "You're entirely welcome."

"I should object. You are too generous. So much meat. And coffee. Even sugar and tinned milk. I really should object to this. But I will not. The children—all the people—will be grateful. As I am too and as my grandfather most assuredly is as well."

How the hell did she know about the contents of the wagon? There hadn't been anything close to time enough for the food to be unload. There'd hardly been time for the wagon to be taken around to the back of the house. Yet Anita was already thanking him for specific items. Dex was baffled. He'd heard that news can travel as quickly as rumor but this was ridiculous.

"Rice and cornmeal can fill a child's belly," he said, "but sometimes a little honey makes the world a happier place, you know."

"You bought honey, too? Now I am impressed. You are thoughtful." She clapped a hand over her mouth with a startled little yelp. "Goodness. Forgive me. Anita and Paco. I did not thank you properly for what you did to help them. We—all of us—we are most grateful for that. It is terrible to think what would have happened."

"You don't have to say anything about that. They've already said everything that was necessary and then some."

"But you must know, señor, that we are in your debt." She glanced over her shoulder toward the house. "Now even more so. You must join us for the evening meal, señor. It would honor us to share this joy with you."

There was enough now that Dex didn't have to worry about the amount of food his presence would cost them.

But he kinda wished Anita had offered him lunch now instead of dinner later. He'd gotten a fairly late start from town, and the heavily burdened mules were slow. Steady but definitely slow. The sun was already sinking past the mid-afternoon point and he hadn't had any lunch yet. Hadn't thought to carry one with him either, although he should have.

"I accept," he said. "With pleasure." Conversation over dinner would also give him a chance to talk with Don Cesar about the threats imposed by Sir David Manchester.

"Would you join me on the patio again, señor? I have asked for refreshments to be brought."

"That sounds nice, thanks."

Among the things he'd bought and brought out this time was a peck of lemons with thick, knobby, bright yellow skins so the family could have their lemonade again.

Dex followed the woman along the now somewhat familiar route around the shaded perimeter of the adobe house to the cool beauty of the bougainvillea-shaded patio.

· 29 ·

Dinner was . . . not what Dex expected. This due to one single glaring omission. Don Cesar was neither seen nor heard from.

The table—at least he'd finally been allowed to set foot inside the sanctum sanctorum and join the family indoors—was set for five. Dex was given a place of honor to the right of the head of the table. Anita sat opposite him next to a very handsome if somewhat foppish gentleman of thirty or thereabouts named Hernando. And Anselma—pretty, sexy, impish Anselma—was seated beside Dex.

The head of the table would naturally be the rightful place for Don Cesar to sit, and plates and silver were laid out there. But when the serving women filled the crystal goblets, that one remained empty. When coffee was poured, Don Cesar's cup was unused. And soon the women began carrying platters and steaming bowls around, always offering the dish first to Dex, then to Anita, then Hernando, and finally to Anselma. The meal had begun and there was still no sign of the old gentleman, nor did anyone else at the table seem to think it strange that Don Cesar did not appear. Apparently everyone but Dexter accepted this without comment.

He, on the other hand, was curious. He smiled across the table—ignoring Anselma's foot, which was gently stroking the side of his right ankle—and said to Anita, "I'd hoped to speak with your grandfather this evening. I take it he won't be joining us?"

"My grandfather is—" She paused and frowned for a moment in thought, then had a whispered consultation with Hernando. "Unwell," Anita said eventually. "He is unwell this evening and, so sorry, cannot join you in this occasion of gratefulness."

"Then please convey to him my regards for his health."

Anita nodded gravely, then turned her head and again whispered something to Hernando. Translating? Dex thought perhaps so although he couldn't hear.

"Would it be possible for me to visit with him in the morning?" Dex asked. He would be staying the night. They'd already prepared a room for him in the wing to the east side of the courtyard patio.

"I am sorry," Anita said. "I do not think that will be so able." She whispered to Hernando again.

Dex doubted the old man had been sick a day in his life and most assuredly never so ill that he would have refused to receive an hidalgo of Spanish blood, Anita's explanations notwithstanding. This brush-off was the same as the first time Dex visited here.

"I respect your grandfather's wishes," Dex said, "and understand that he might not want to visit with someone who is beneath his station. Where I come from, my own family had privilege and what you might consider to be rank. I ask to see him only because the things I wish to discuss are important. To all of you who live here."

Anita whispered to Hernando. Then turned to Dex and with a patently false smile said, "Let us not ruin our meal with such serious words, neh? We will speak of these things later."

"With Don Cesar?" Dex pressed.

Anita only shrugged.

Hernando tugged at her elbow beneath the level of the tabletop. He kept his hand low so that Dex could not see, but the cloth of Anita's sleeve dipped and tightened like a cork bobber floating on the waters of the Mississippi when a catfish took the bait, giving Hernando's game away.

The handsome fellow held his napkin to his lips as if wiping something from his mouth and probably whispered something. Dex could not hear what. But then Hernando could have shouted it and Dex wouldn't have understood a word of the Spanish anyway. They were only trying to be polite though. Dex knew that and took no offense.

"Would you care for more of the chicken, Mr. Yancey?"

"Thank you; that would be nice." He had no idea what the dish was, but the pieces of breast meat were tender, swimming in a mildly spicy sauce that was so good Dex could have eaten it as a soup.

Anita motioned to one of the servants, then Dex's plate was quickly refilled.

Actually, though, now that his immediate hunger was satisfied his interest lay more in the promise inherent in Anselma's continual rubbing and stroking.

He was certain the servants on that side of the dining

room could see what she was doing. After all, the table-cloth did not fall to floor length, and Selma was blatant enough about her attentions.

If she didn't mind, though, Dex saw no reason he should.

Good manners prevented him from returning the show of affection. But that didn't mean he wasn't interested. He was only worried about how it would look when the meal ended and he had to remove the napkin from his lap. It would likely look like he was trying to steal some of the heavy, ornate silverware by stuffing a carving knife into his britches. Or a tent pole. Thinking about little Selma had him horny as three billygoats.

"More wine, señor?" Anita offered.

"No, thank you." He wanted all of his faculties to remain intact. For later in the night.

✦ 30 ✦

An evening of genteel conversation among strangers can be dull enough when everyone speaks a common tongue. With Dex isolated by his lack of Spanish, the boredom was excruciating.

He suffered through a skit put on by a troupe of children aged five or so through eight or maybe nine, listened to three little girls in the ten-to-twelve age bracket offer recital pieces on a badly out-of-tune piano and politely smiled his way through an undoubtedly wonderful medley of song performed by a quartet of young men.

Dex knew it was a medley only because Anita told him so. He did, however, recognize one word in the lyrics. "Si" was used fairly often, and Dex had it on good authority that that meant "yes". Sadly, that was not enough Spanish to enable him to enjoy the spirited performance.

When the evening's entertainment ended—mercifully— Dex accepted still more thanks from a delegation of the hacienda children and watched everyone drift away from the music room until only the same close family members who had been at the dinner table remained.

"It is late, señor," Anita said, "and the day has been long." She smiled. "It has been wonderful thanks to you, but we are becoming weary. You would to please excuse?"

"I'd hoped to have a word with Don Cesar," Dex said.

"So sorry. Perhaps tomorrow."

Sure, he thought. And if not tomorrow then maybe on the sixth Tuesday of next January. He'd count on that.

"Perhaps," he said politely. He hesitated. "I hope you will at least inform Don Cesar that I have information that would be helpful to him."

"Of course," Anita said with a smile so angelic and in a voice so syrup-sweet that Dex knew damned good and well the woman was lying through her teeth.

"You are very kind."

The smile remained. Hernando stood, bowed low, and said something in Spanish that Anita did not bother to translate. It was quite obviously an effusive and meaningless expression of good night. Dex returned the bow and the conventional phrases, then accepted a curtsy and rather more heartfelt good night from Anselma.

"If you are ready to retire, Mr. Yancey?" Anita asked when everyone but one lingering maidservant was gone.

"Thank you."

"Then I shall show you to your room."

He followed her through a hallway, across the now torchlit patio and into the far wing of the low, rambling, very old house. It was a good thing he had a guide or he couldn't possibly have gotten there.

Anita stopped at the door and told him, "Leave your clothing on the—I think the word is valette?" He nodded.

Close enough. "And please to leave your door unbolted. Someone will come in while you sleep to gather your things. They will be made fresh and pressed ready for you in the morning, neh?"

"You don't have to do that."

"It is our custom. Please. It would be," she stopped and seemed to be groping for the word, "it would be an affront to my grandfather to refuse."

"I would not wish to offend him."

"Good." She hesitated again, then said, "Yes, well, please you will have a night of comfort, yes?"

"Yes," he agreed readily enough. After the way that little mink Anselma acted at supper he suspected the night would be more tiring than comforting. But he would be willing to bear up under the strain if it came to that.

Anita peeped inside the room to make sure the bedside table lamp was lighted and trimmed to a low flame, that the thick comforter had been turned down on the massive, canopied bed—the style of the bed was what Dex would have called a sleigh bed had it originated in a colder climate than this one, but then what did he know about Mexican or Spanish furnishings—and that the room seemed in comfortable readiness for an honored guest.

Satisfied then, she offered her hand for a prim shake, lifted her skirts, and disappeared toward some distant part of the house.

At least Dex hoped everyone else would remain at some distance. With this big bed to wrestle in and those tedious hours of waiting to make up for, he didn't want to have to hold anything back when Anselma showed up.

And leave the door open so someone could come fetch his clothes? That instruction was entirely unnecessary. He wouldn't have thought of bolting it tonight.

He hurriedly undressed, arranged his clothes on the shaped wooden rack provided beside the entry then climbed into the tall bed and extinguished the lamp.

Now if only Anselma would hurry her pretty little butt along . . .

· 31 ·

Dex heard the creak of seldom-used hinges and the soft padding of bare feet on tile and then, closer, on the thick woolen rug that was laid out at the side of his bed.

He felt a slight shift in the angle of the mattress as a small body joined him on the bed.

He smelled a faint and very delicate fragrance. Citrus, he thought. His nose wrinkled. He wasn't sure but thought perhaps, just perhaps this scent was the zest of a lemon's skin.

He saw . . . nothing. The room was bathed in darkness.

He heard a sigh. Felt the sheet pulled back at his side. Became instantly aware of the warmth of a body lying very close beside his. Felt the brush of hot breath on the suddenly very sensitive skin at the side of his neck. Felt a gentle, exploring hand. The wet, delightful probe of a tongue tip into the cup of his ear and—painful but amazingly arousing—the sharp, unexpected nip of teeth clamp suddenly onto his earlobe and as quickly withdrawn.

Dex gasped. Rolled onto his side. His inquiring hand found soft skin and the dip of a tiny waist, the swell of a woman's rounded hip. He leaned forward, encountered a fluttering eyelash, adjusted his aim downward from that reference point and tasted the soft, sweet flavors of generous lips and a probing tongue.

Dex groaned aloud as his roving hand slid up the laddered ribcage to the swell of ripe, full breasts.

A hand cupped his balls, then played teasingly up and down the length of his shaft.

He withdrew his tongue and whispered, "Suck me."

She did better than that. She kissed him again, then very slowly and very, very thoroughly began to lick and suckle lower, lower, lower.

He nearly wasted his juices on the bedding when she began to lick and nibble at his right nipple, then onto his left. Every renewed pull of sweet suction on his nipple led to a bouncing, throbbing response from his cock.

"Now," he croaked. "I can't wait much longer. Suck me now."

She giggled very, very softly. Then he felt her weight shift as she left his chest and snuggled tight against his body at waist level.

Wet heat enveloped him, and she sucked so hard he was afraid she would pull his kneecaps onto his hips.

Dex groaned and arched his back, driving himself hard into her mouth. There was a moment of resistance and he could both hear and feel her gag at the intrusion.

But after no more than a heartbeat or two she relaxed her throat and admitted him all the way. He could feel the tip of her nose pressing against his balls.

She withdrew then and he thought she was pulling away. Instead she only made a slight change in the angle of her body, then drove down hard with her body to impale herself on his cock, the sensitive head of his prick extending inside her throat while her teeth lightly rested against the base of his shaft.

Dex began to buck wildly up and down. He couldn't help it. The feel of her, taking all of him like that, engulfing him, surrounding every last bit of surface area—it was almost more than he could bear.

He cried out—loudly—with an explosive spasm of pleasure as hot, sticky fluids gushed out of his loins and into her belly.

She stayed with him for long, splendid seconds, then very slowly withdrew while continuing to maintain the suction with her lips wrapped tight around him.

When wet, weary flesh finally popped into the cool night air, she sighed and, laughing, bent to take him once more between her lips. But tenderly this time, delicately sipping from the tip end of him so that she could draw the last possible droplets of semen from his body.

At length she pulled away and spent though he was Dex hated to lose the pleasure of feeling her skin against his.

"I didn't know anybody could be that good," he said. "You should've told me before that you knew how to do that, my dear." He sighed. "Damn but you're an almighty good fuck." He shook his head. "Sure do wish I knew how to tell you that in Spanish."

"I am as 'appy to hear it in the English, no? An' I thank you for saying these things to me, Señor Yancey of the Estadas Unidas."

"What the—?"

◆ 32 ◆

"Anita, I thought you were—" He'd thought she was Anselma, of course. But he couldn't exactly *say* that, never mind that Anita probably knew it full well. After all, it wasn't exactly a secret that he'd been with Anselma in town that night. The family might not know about the wagon ride the other day, but they all would damned sure know about the old man and Anselma's five dollar gold piece.

"I thought you were in bed," he finished lamely.

She laughed and bit the point of his chin, then softened her punishment by kissing him. He could smell the sea-salt scent of his own cum on her breath.

"What was that for?"

She didn't answer. Didn't have to.

And the fact was that Anita was the better of the two in bed. Of course he couldn't say that either. But it was true.

"I thought . . . I mean, I don't like to bring up an unpleasant subject, but won't Hernando wonder where you are right now?"

"You fear he will burst in to demand—how is it you say—satisfaction?" Anita didn't sound at all concerned. But then in fairness to her she didn't sound either like the sort of girl who likes to pit one male admirer against another just for the joy of seeing them fight over her.

"No," Dex said honestly enough. "It isn't fear on my part that worries me but concern for your reputation. I wouldn't want you to get into trouble with your husband, after all."

Anita began to laugh again.

"Something funny?" Dex asked.

"*Si*," she said. "You. You think Nando, he is my husband?"

"I, uh . . . yeah. I do. I mean . . . I did?"

"My husban', that no good, he married me for my own good name and my grandpappa's good money. You know the kind?"

"I know the kind," Dex agreed.

"I send him away long time agone."

"But Hernando—?"

He could feel Anita shrug, although the room was much too dark for him to see her.

"Nando, he is a cousin only. An' he would not care if you fock me on top the dining room table. 'Ey, he might enjoy to watch. But it would not be me he would want to see naked."

"I don't under . . . oh. Never mind."

Anita chuckled. "Poor Nando is not interested in girls, an' he is too afraid of grandpappa to harm little boys. I think he must settle for his own hand. Or for the sheep."

Dex damn near swallowed his tongue on that one. Anita, for all her haughty ways, could be downright earthy when she wanted to.

He kissed the girl again and pulled her close against his side. The scent and the feel of her was beginning to arouse him again.

And Anita hadn't yet had any pleasure for herself. She'd pleased him and then some. But she herself hadn't so much as had a fingertip poking into the gateway to a lady's happiness.

Dex was going to have to do something to correct that oversight. That, after all, would be the gentlemanly thing to do.

◆ 33 ◆

The bedroom door swung open, admitting a spill of light from the hallway. Dex froze in place. Which was not an easy thing to do at that exact moment. He was lying in the saddle, mounted on top of Anita with her arms and legs wrapped tight around him while he drilled deep inside her.

The light, he quickly saw, came from a small bulls-eye lantern in the hand of a short, fat woman whose feet were muffled in layers of cloth so she could move about on the tiled floor without making noise. She'd damn sure done that so far. Dex hadn't heard her coming. He'd heard Anita coming—well, in a slightly different meaning of the word—several times already. But not this intruder.

The fat woman's attention, fortunately, was focused on the wooden valet where Dex's clothing hung. She bent down and placed the lantern on the floor while she gathered his things and draped them over her arm, then picked up the lantern again and slipped out into the hallway as silently as she'd arrived.

So far as Dex could tell she never once glanced toward the bed or noticed that it was occupied. Or just exactly *how* it was being occupied.

Once the door was safely shut again Dex could feel Anita's belly begin to quiver and tremble beneath his.

It took him a moment to realize why. She was laughing. The woman was ever so quietly cracking up with laughter.

The sense of amusement was contagious. Dex began to laugh, too. And then both of them burst into loud guffaws while he continued to lie on top of her, his cock still socketed within her.

Dex laughed until tears came and he was gasping for breath, and he knew Anita was doing the same. Even so, he managed to maintain his penetration. And as the laughter waned, the rippling movements of Anita's belly began to renew his state of arousal.

His hard-on, which may have sagged just the least little bit while they were distracted, came raging insistently back, and he kissed her fiercely while once more commencing to stroke and drive.

Anita's attention turned fully to that sensation again too and she clutched at him, planting her calves behind Dex's thighs and yanking him all the deeper with every downstroke he delivered so that his belly slammed with punishing strength onto her smaller, softer body. She acted as if she couldn't get enough, as if no amount of battering would be too much for her to take.

And moments before Dex's explosion, Anita began to shudder and groan in one violent release after another un-

til both of them collapsed in exhaustion with Dex still
lying atop Anita's limp body.

The bedroom door swung open, admitting a spill of light
from the hallway. Dex froze in place. He continued to lie
on top of Anita, both of them half asleep . . . and the other
half quite completely spent and satisfied.

He glanced toward the doorway. Again the bulls-eye
lantern. Again someone standing beside the valet.

Not the fat woman this time though. This person was
much smaller. He could see that much but little more as
the lantern was carried low.

And this time instead of the light being shined on a
clothes rack it was turned toward the bed, glaring in Dex's
eyes. He blinked.

Anita gasped.

There was another, almost perfectly matching gasp of
surprise from the doorway.

Anita let out a burst of Spanish.

And so did the person in the . . . Anselma. It was Anselma's voice coming from behind the lantern.

The girl had come to him after all. Dex didn't know if
he should feel flattered now or . . . well, he wasn't sure
just what was going on.

The one thing he knew for certain sure was that Anita
and Anselma were going at it hammer and tongs while
Anita still lay on the bed with Dexter for a blanket.

While the two of them snarled and spat at each other,
Dex rolled off Anita and fumbled for the long-forgotten
sheet to cover himself with.

Anita was having none of the sheet. As soon as Dex
was off her she jumped up and advanced on Anselma.

Anita, Dex noted, had one almighty fine body. He'd

been enjoying the feel and the use of it for quite some time now, but this was the first chance he'd had to observe it. The girl had great legs and a world-class ass. Nice tits too. Bigger than Anselma's. Not quite so firm.

Anselma, either because of neglect or out of some perverse impulse, kept the lantern light shining on Anita's naked body. Dex damn sure didn't mind that, and apparently neither one of them did either.

For a minute or so there Dex thought the two women were going to get into a scratch-and-claw hair pulling catfight. Hissing and spitting was as far as it got.

He did kinda wish he could understand what they were saying though. Could've been damned flattering. Or on the other hand . . . Maybe it was just as well he didn't know.

After five or six minutes of this verbal combat—it was a wonder the whole household wasn't aroused, because once they were launched into it, neither girl bothered to keep her voice down—Anselma said something that from her tone of voice Dex suspected was a really, really scathing parting shot, then turned on her heels and stomped out of the room.

Took the lantern with her, of course, which Dex thought was something of a shame. He'd been enjoying the view.

Anselma left the door standing wide open—deliberately, he was sure—so Anita closed and this time bolted it—Dex could hear the sound of the bolt sliding home—then returned to the bed where Dex would be able to comfort and soothe her.

Plenty of hugging and kissing, he realized, would be in order right now.

As for Anselma, well, there wasn't much he could do

about that. At this moment. But hell, maybe the younger girl would want some soothing too in the future.

Dex pulled Anita close and began to stroke and gentle her.

• 34 •

There were only two pillows on the bed. Both were propped behind Dex so he could recline with all the comfort of a pasha. Anita didn't need a pillow. She had Dex's shoulder to lie on. He held her there in the circle of his right arm while with his left hand he toyed with her hair. He was comfortable now. Sated to the point that he might not be able to get a hard-on again for days. Or hours. Or, well, for several minutes, anyhow. He yawned.

"You are sleepy," Anita said.

Dex shook his head. "Not really. I'm enjoying myself too much to want to waste time sleeping."

"You are not sorry I came to you?"

"I'm glad." He smiled and bent his head far enough so he could lightly kiss her forehead. "Thought I'd already showed you how glad."

If Anita'd been a cat she would have started purring. He could tell she was pleased. Didn't have to have light enough to see her. He could feel her pleasure in the quiet, trusting way she lay close beside him and in the gentle stroking touch of her fingertips along his upper thigh.

"Anita."

"Yes, dear one?"

"In the morning—"

"The morning will come too soon." She pouted. "I do not want to talk about the morning."

"The morning will come, yes, and so will other nights. But tomorrow morning, Anita, I need to see your grandfather. I need to speak with him."

"Grandpappa will not speak with you, Dexter. So sorry, but this is true. He is ver' proud man, my grandpappa. He does not want to think that you have lain with his granddaughter. Oh! How he would turn his head away from us if he knew you have lain with this granddaughter, too. It would be a most terrible thing, Dexter. You have been good to us, to all of us, that is so true. But grandpappa is so ver' proud. You know? He will not speak with you. He will not see you. He will pretend to not know you are in this house, even. Can you understand this thing I say?"

Dex stroked her hair some more. "I understand better than you realize, Anita. Your grandfather is very much like mine. They speak different languages, but I think they are much alike. Very proud. Very correct."

"Correct. Yes, that is a good word. Correct. It is important to Grandpappa that things be correct."

"I have to talk with him, Anita."

"You will not see him again, Dexter. This he will not do."

"But I have to, Anita."

"It is not possible."

"Not even to save the Espinosa ranch?"

Anita turned onto her side and reached up to touch Dex's cheek. "You are a generous man, my dear Dexter, but you do not have enough money to save this rancho. More than a few dollars that would require."

"But that's what I want to tell your grandfather, Anita. I *can* do something to keep David Manchester from taking your family's land holdings."

"You know this Manchester person?" Anita asked.

"Honey, that's what I need to tell your granddaddy. Yes, I know Manchester. In fact, he thinks I'm going to help him get your land. But I'm not. What I intend to do, dear, is just the opposite. I want to help your grandfather beat Manchester."

"I do not understand," Anita said.

"I'll tell you what. Let me explain it all to you. Then you can tell your granddaddy and maybe then he'll agree to see me so he and I can work out a plan to defeat David Manchester once and for all."

Anita sat upright and after a moment, he felt the tilt of the bed as she stood up. He could hear her fumbling about in the dark, then the bright flare of a match momentarily blinded him. When he could see again Anita—Lordy, but she was one fine-looking woman, even better looking naked than when clothed and there were damned few women who could make that claim—was lighting a small lamp on the bedside table.

"I want to see your face when you speak to me of these things," Anita said, her voice oddly cold now. "I will see the truth in your eyes, Dexter. If you lie to me of these thing, I myself will claw those eyes from your face and slice your manhood into scraps to feed the dog."

"You don't have to get all that dramatic about it," he said.

"I do not embroider upon this," she said. He kind of thought she meant to say embellish instead of embroider. But then what the hell did he know about Mexican women and their pledges. "*Es verdad*," she said. "It is true."

"Then pull that chair over and look close," he told her, "because what I'm going to tell you is straight from the horse's mouth."

She frowned. "Straight from where?"

"I just mean to say that it's true. What was the word you used? *Verdad*? All right then. It's pure *verdad*, through and through. So sit yourself down, look as close into my eyes as you like, and listen to what I want to tell your grandfather tomorrow morning."

Dex stood, as good manners dictated, but was disappointed to see that it was Anselma who was joining them in the dining room and not Anita.

One of the servants had come to fetch him a little earlier, but his only breakfast companion so far was Hernando, and with no English, Hernando made for rather poor company.

Anselma, he saw, seemed to have come to grips with the fact that he'd spent the past night with Anita in his bed and not herself.

Still, it was obvious the girl was willing to dispute her elder sister for Dexter's affections. This morning she was dressed as if for a soiree with her hair piled high, her gown a thing of grandeur—or would have been a generation ago; God knew what ancient trunk or storeroom she'd dragged it from—and gaudy dangling earrings big enough to serve as snaffle bits.

Dex rather preferred the gay and elfin Anselma he'd

come to know so well before. But he wouldn't for anything have told her that and spoiled her attempts to become a femme fatale.

She was dressed to do battle and so he bowed and exclaimed at her beauty and never mind the language barrier. He figured a woman can always comprehend the intent of a compliment whether she understood the words or not.

Hernando ignored his little cousin and continued to spear bits of sliced melon from a silver platter in front of him while Dex did the honors of seating Anselma beside him.

He couldn't help glancing frequently through the double-doored entry, however, and out into the hallway. He wanted to see Anselma, dammit, but there'd been no sign of her since the break of dawn when she gave him a final passionate kiss and slipped silently out of his room.

That would have been something like three hours past and already he was growing horny again. There was something about Anita . . .

Anselma barely had time to begin rubbing Dex's ankle with her foot when a young man appeared in the doorway motioning for Dexter to join him.

Dex excused himself—Anselma looked disappointed; Hernando ignored him—and went out into the hallway.

Good, he was thinking. Anita's done it. He would finally have that chance to meet with the old man. He needed to tell Don Cesar about Manchester's plans and come up with something to counter them.

"D'you speak English?" he asked his guide as they wended through a series of narrow, dark hallways that quickly had Dex completely lost.

The guide shrugged and placed his hands over his ears. Drat. No English, Dex thought.

The guide forged ahead at a rapid pace.

The last passageway brought them into a slightly musty lean-to and from there into a hot and noisy small building set a little way apart from what Dex judged to be the back wall of the sprawling hacienda.

Loudly chattering women were busy tending a pair of brick stoves while off to one side, pale smoke drifted from a beehive-shaped adobe oven. A handful of small children sat in a corner playing with a litter of kittens barely old enough to have their eyes open. The room was filled with the smells of woodsmoke and food. Strings of colorful dried peppers hung from the rafters on one side while on the other Dex could see hams and bacon slabs that he recognized from his shopping excursion in town the day before.

The kitchen. He'd been brought through the service alleys to the kitchen. He was—

Dammit! He was being dismissed. Not only sent packing but sent packing in such a way as to be deliberately insulting. He was being sent off as if a servant himself.

Anita wouldn't have done such a thing. He knew that. Hell, she probably didn't even know about it.

But her grandfather did. This insult was Don Cesar's not very subtle way of telling him to leave this family alone. He was being sent away and as good as told outright that he should not return.

If Anita'd had a chance to tell the old man what Dex told her last night surely this would not have happened.

He could go back inside. Find Don Cesar. Get the old man to listen to him. He could—

What he probably could *not* do was get anywhere near the inside of the hacienda again.

Well, not without a fistfight at the very least.

When he realized what was up here and turned around, his guide was behind him blocking the doorway that led back inside the house, and the other doors on that side of the kitchen were also blocked. It looked like the entire young male population of the rancho had been brought in to stand there with their arms crossed over scrawny chests so they could keep Dex out.

There wasn't a one of them that Dex couldn't whip. He was pretty sure about that. Hell, he could probably take on three or four of them if need be. But there weren't one. Or three. Or four.

He could see at least eight—no, nine—of them now. Even if he wanted to start something here—and he did not—it would serve no purpose.

But . . . dammit—

The young man who'd just brought him out said something to him in a soft voice. There was pain in the young man's eyes. Dex gathered that this young fellow would do as he'd been told. But he suspected the order was not popular. These pleasant and hospitable people felt an obligation to Dexter and did not want to disappoint him. Now they were told to be deliberately rude to him and make him leave.

It wasn't their fault, Dex reminded himself.

If he could only talk to Anita . . . if Anselma only understood English. Neither girl was anywhere in sight now.

The women who were here were averting their eyes so as not to humiliate him any further. That was damned kind of them and he appreciated it.

The kids hadn't been let in on the adults' instructions.

Several of them saw him and abandoned the kittens to run to him and gather around his legs, laughing and touching in the innocent way little ones have of expressing open and joyous affection.

The hell with the idea of insult. Instead of hurrying away like a cur in the night he took his time about bending down and giving a word of greeting and encouragement to each of the children in turn. He spoke to them, looked into their guileless eyes, ruffled their hair and touched their cheeks, then doffed his hat to the ladies and, ignoring the platoon of young men sent to guard him, strode out into the morning sunshine.

As he'd already expected, the now empty freight wagon was standing ready for him, the team already in harness and being held by a pair of young boys.

Dex thanked the kids who were holding the horses and climbed into the driving box whistling a light tune he'd heard once in a New Orleans brothel.

Don Cesar might be able to throw him out, but he'd be damned if the old man would get him down, too.

Dex clucked to the livery stable team and drove away from the hacienda with his chin held high and his determination to help these people undiminished. The hell with arrogant men, young or old, British or Mexican. Dexter would do what he thought was right and piss on the rest of it.

• 36 •

W here the hell was James now that Dex needed him? Damn it, anyway. If James were here Dex was sure he would have no problem working this out. James would be able to make eyes at one of those South African girls out at the Victoria Cross and get a complete report on everything Manchester did, ate or—hell—thought about.

Besides, James had a good head on his shoulders. For their whole lives long any time one of them had a problem he could turn to the other for help. Between them virtually any difficulty seemed a snap to overcome.

Until now.

James, dammit, was somewhere off on a jaunt to see his mama.

Not that Dex blamed him. Dex only wished he could do the same thing. Except of course Dex had neither a mother—whom he'd never known, anyway—nor a father to go back to. And he certainly wasn't anxious to have another visit with his backstabbing, inheritance-stealing dear brother Lewis. Not now, not ever.

But James . . . Dex sighed. He really did wish James was here now. And for more than just James's ability to spy on the Manchester household, more than the contribution of James's good sense.

This was the first time in Dex's memory that the two had been apart, and Dex just plain missed the black-assed son of a bitch.

Dex thought grumpily about that and about Don Cesar and about Sir David Francis Manchester and none of those subjects did much toward bringing joy to his heart or a spring into his step.

He got back to Huaca Guadalupe well past noon and turned the wagon in at the livery, checked on the well-being of his horse, and then headed straight for the café. His breakfast had been interrupted this morning and he was hungry again.

With so little sleep the night before—not that he was complaining, considering the reason why he'd been somewhat too busy to waste time sleeping—and with his belly full, Dex returned to the hotel and stretched out for an afternoon nap.

But before he lay down, he crossed to the window and carefully arranged the shade so that it covered only half the window opening.

That allowed a mildly uncomfortable amount of sunlight to spill into the room, but that was unimportant at the moment. He wanted to summon Ambrose Clay to another clandestine meeting tonight.

It had occurred to him on the drive back to town that

if he couldn't convince Don Cesar Espinosa to cooperate in Manchester's destruction, then perhaps his best course of action would be to seek help from another source.

The source of assistance he had in mind was none other than Sir David Francis Manchester.

• 37 •

"I need information," Dex told Clay when the lawyer showed up late at the corral.

"That's what you called me out here for? So you could ask me for help? I thought you'd be reporting your progress to Sir David. If you made any progress, that is."

"We'll get to that later. What I need now, Clay, is information. And since you grew up here and know the way things are around here, you should be able to fill me in on some things."

"Why didn't you ask your dear friend Don Cesar?" Clay countered.

"Your jealousy is showing," Dex told him. "Unless there is some other reason you're dragging your feet about a few simple questions."

"You didn't answer mine," the lawyer pointed out.

"That's right, and I don't have to. Sir David made it plain enough which of us was in charge here, and it doesn't happen to be you. Which is probably the reason your nose is so far out of joint. Not that I give a damn about that. Don't mind telling you why I want to ask these things of you instead of Espinosa either.

"The reason, mister, is because I want to come across with him as being helpful and friendly but with no particular inquisitiveness. Certainly I don't want to say or do anything that would hint that I might have a vested interest in what happens between him and Sir David. As far as Espinosa is concerned I want to be the friendly listener. Period.

"But when he does bring something up in conversation, I want to know what he's talking about so I can offer intelligent suggestions without having to dwell on long explanations. Can you understand my reasoning here?"

"I suppose so," Clay grudgingly acknowledged. "What is it that you want to know?"

"I want to know as much as I can about Don Cesar's rancho. He raises sheep, right?"

"That's right."

"I know less than nothing about sheep and how to raise them. I need to learn. At the very least I need to know what would affect Sir David's plan and Don Cesar's ability to hold out against him."

"This is going to take a while, and I don't want to stand here ankle deep in mule shit while we talk. Could we go up to your room instead? I can go in through the back door without being seen."

"Are you sure?"

"He keeps it unlocked so guests can go out to the shitter during the night. I'm sure."

"Sounds like you've done this before," Dex said.

"You aren't the only one who likes to get a little pussy on the sly, Yancey."

"Married, are you?"

Clay shrugged. "What she doesn't know can't hurt her."

"You know the room," Dex said. "I'll leave the door open."

"I'll be right behind you."

Clay was as good as his word. About that, anyway. Dex hadn't any more than gotten the bedside lamp lighted than the door silently opened and Brose Clay came inside. Dex motioned his "guest" to the straight-backed chair beside the window. He himself sat on the side of the bed.

"Sheep," Clay mused, his attention focused not on Dexter but on his own fingernails, which he inspected one by one. "They do pretty well in this country. Do you know anything about raising cattle?"

"No. But I could teach you how to raise cotton."

Clay made a sour face. "No thanks. I'm not interested in any of these things that make you sweat."

"You were saying?"

"Right. Sheep. Cattle graze. Sheep browse."

Dex was not entirely sure of the difference, but he didn't interrupt now that Clay was talking.

"You can raise five, maybe six sheep on the same amount of land that it takes to raise one cow. And of course you get two crops from the sheep, both the lambs for meat and the wool that sells separately. You make more money from sheep than from cattle."

"Then why would Sir David want to raise cattle here if the land is better suited to sheep?" Dex asked.

Clay gave him a rather disgusted look, then looked down at his hands again. "Pride. Decency. Manhood. Sheep are vile, smelly creatures. Real men appreciate fine horses and raise cattle."

That too was a distinction that escaped Dex's comprehension. Well, except for the part about fine horses. He could appreciate a blooded mount or a dog with a rich voice as well as the next man. But why sheep should be detestable and cattle desirable . . . that part he didn't understand.

"Either one of them," Clay was continuing, "needs water. This is dry country, so anything living will need a steady supply of water. Sir David understands that. His first act was to buy up, appropriate, or fence off as much water as he could. He accomplished that before old Don Cesar realized what his new neighbor was up to."

"And then?"

"Then Sir David hired—never mind exactly who he hired, that part isn't important—he made sure Don Cesar's sheepherders wouldn't be getting in the way."

"You say 'made sure'," Dex said. "How sure?"

Clay looked at him for a moment and said, "Dead sure."

"He had some of Don Cesar's men killed?" Dex asked.

"I didn't say that."

"No, but I'm asking it. I have to know just how well the old man has been softened up. And how much resistance I have to overcome out there."

Clay hesitated. But he had little choice about it. Dex's reasoning was sound. And Sir David Manchester had instructed him to cooperate with Dex as their man inside the Espinosa household. "Only three of them were killed. Maybe two or three others wounded. They started to get the idea after that. They knew if they came out onto the range and tried to take their sheep to water they'd be in peril. Not too many of them tried after that."

"That's why all those wagons are parked and empty at the rancho?"

Clay nodded.

"What happened to the sheep?"

"Damned if I'd know. We shot some of them."

He'd said 'we', Dex noticed. It sounded to him like Ambrose Clay had used a rifle himself and not only his men. Dex couldn't help wondering if that included during the shooting of Don Cesar's sheepherders or if the lawyer left that part of it to his underlings.

Not that Dex expected a lawyer to have any scruples, but he supposed some of them might have weaker stomachs than others.

"What about the rest?" Dex asked.

Clay shrugged. "They scattered. Likely died. A sheep isn't anything but a creature looking for an excuse to die anyhow. With no water and no sheepherders to protect them and no dogs to take care of them, I wouldn't think very many are still living. God only knows where they'd be, the ones that might still be alive."

"You shot dogs, too?" Dex asked.

"Had to. A good sheepdog can take care of a flock even without a sheepherder to guide them. Getting rid of the dogs was almost as important as getting rid of the sheepherders."

It took all of Dex's self-control to keep his expression neutral and his voice calm. He didn't know or care all that much about cattle or sheep either one. But dogs?

Damn any louse-ridden son of a bitch who'd shoot a dog.

"So Espinosa might still have some sheep out on the range at this point?" Dex asked when he had control of himself again.

"Oh, he probably does. Not so many as before, but I'd say there are still some out there."

"But the longer Sir David controls the water and keeps the sheepherders bottled up, the worse off the Espinosas will be."

"That's right."

"And where do you come in?"

Clay sat up straighter in the chair and puffed his chest with self-importance. "I'm the one who can make sure it all comes in on the clear side of the law. A little tinkering with the records here, a few bribes there . . . Sir David doesn't have to worry about coming out of this as the legal owner of the water rights he needs. He just has to break the old man and keep him too cash short to mount a defense."

"I see," Dex said. And so he did. It was beginning to make sense to him now. "What about Sir David? I take it he has the financial resources to carry his plan through as far as necessary?"

"Sir David is well backed by investors in England. High-born, important people. Titled people, you see."

"Uh huh." Dex was thinking that if . . . dammit. There was a kernel of an idea there somewhere. But was like a round seed on a flat table. He could see it; he just couldn't pick it up and hold it in his hand. Quite.

"I'm glad we've had this talk," Dex said, setting the thoughts aside to germinate in their own good time. "You're a big help."

"What are you going to do next?" Clay asked.

"I think tomorrow I'll ride out to see Sir David."

"Do you want me to go with you?"

"No, I still don't think we should be seen together. But I'll be riding out in the morning. I'll leave town heading east, then circle back to pick up the road to the Victoria

Cross. If you want to meet us there around noontime, that would be your privilege."

"I'll be there," Clay said.

Which Dex had expected anyway. He wouldn't have thought Clay would allow him access to Manchester without Clay there to listen in and perhaps to undermine. The lawyer was not exactly a close ally, and Dex knew he would be well advised to watch his backside when Clay was around.

"Tomorrow," Dex said, standing and extending a hand to make sure Clay knew their little visit was over now.

Clay hesitated for half a heartbeat, then accepted the offered handshake. Dex took care to lock the hotel room door behind him.

⋄ 38 ⋄

Dex climbed down from the saddle and tossed his reins to the young Negro who'd come rushing to greet him with a set of wooden steps, which Dexter ignored. He wasn't to the point of wanting steps to mount and dismount regardless of David Manchester's notions of the way gentlepersons should be pampered by their servants.

"Has Mr. Clay arrived yet?"

Dex wasn't sure if the boy responded to his question with a statement or if he was simply clearing his throat. If it was a language it was one Dex never heard before.

"Thanks." He left horse and boy behind and strode to the door where he was greeted by a stunningly pretty girl with skin as dark as midnight and a smile that would make stars blush for the shame of being out-shined.

"I'd like to see Sir David."

"The master is expecting you. Come this way, please." The girl's English was as good as Dexter's but tinged with something of a British accent. The accent sounded odd coming from a black girl, but then what did Dex know about South Africa.

Manchester and Clay were seated in the mansion's library.

"Ah, Mr. Yancey. Our friend Mr. Clay tells me you've been busy on my behalf."

"Yes, I have."

"Excellent. Simply excellent. Will you have some wine to whet your appetite before we dine?"

"No, thank you, but a whiskey would be nice."

"Of course. At once. Please sit, Mr. Yancey. Here will do." Manchester clapped his hands, and another girl, younger if not so pretty as the one who'd been at the entrance, came running for instruction. The tumbler of whiskey—Scotch; Dex would have preferred Irish—was brought almost before Dex had time to settle into the chair at Manchester's immediate right.

Clay, he noticed, had been given a seat somewhat further from the center of power here. Dex was sure Clay was all too well aware of that too and could be counted on to resent the fact.

"Now," Manchester said eagerly, "I understand you spent the night inside the Espinosa house. You are on good terms with him still?"

Dex found that comment very interesting. He hadn't mentioned anything to Ambrose Clay about his sleeping arrangements. And Dex was reasonably sure he himself was not being watched. He would surely have noticed that. He suspected then that it was the hacienda that was being spied on.

In fairness he had to admit that he'd ordered Clay to withdraw the blockade on the road to the hacienda. He didn't recall telling the man anything about not spying on

the place. And really it was just as well. The fact that he'd
been invited to stay overnight was sure to bolster his
standing with Manchester.

Of course, if Manchester ever found out that the old
man refused to receive him . . . Dex hoped Manchester did
not have any spies inside the hacienda compound because
that was the sort of thing that would be certain to cause
gossip in the community of family and employees.

Dex took a swallow of the Scotch whiskey and smiled.
"The old gentleman was truly grateful for the load of
foodstuffs you sent, Sir David." And hell, that was probably true. The smile turned into a grin. "You will forgive
me, I hope, if I failed to mention to him that you were
the source of that good fortune."

Manchester laughed. Brose Clay managed some sounds
that would pass for laughter also.

"And your plan, Mr. Yancey?" Manchester continued.

"My first step will be to deepen the relationship between Don Cesar and myself, of course. He must trust me
first. Then . . . in order to protect him from you, you understand . . . someone in his own family—I'm not yet sure
exactly who—will suggest to him that as an Anglo I
might be able to protect his interests by taking legal control of the water resources."

Dex looked at Clay and said, "You could arrange for
that to be in my name as easily as in Sir David's couldn't
you, Mr. Clay?"

It was an idea that had occurred to him during the night.
He awakened this morning with it already in mind.

"Why . . . yes. I suppose I could at that," Clay said.

"Wonderful," Manchester exclaimed, jumping from his
chair with a childlike display of excitement and clapping
his hands. "What a perfectly marvelous idea. You let the

old man think you want control so you can assure him of access. But how will you make him think you can secure my cooperation, Mr. Yancey?"

"Why, with money, of course. I'll make a cash offer to you."

"The Espinosas no longer have that kind of money, Mr. Yancey. I've seen to that. They keep too many workers on, you see. Treat this like a family instead of the business that it is. They were on a thin margin to begin with. Missing out on their usual receipts for wool sales and lambs shipped to the eastern markets has stripped them of all the cash they might have had in hand. They are virtually destitute. Believe me about this, sir. I have looked into their accounts rather closely, and I know."

Dex grinned again. "But don't you see, Sir David, that is part of my plan. You will buy yourself out."

Manchester frowned. "I don't get that part of it, Mr. Yancey. Please enlighten me."

"You will buy yourself out, Sir David, by offering Don Cesar a mortgage against his land holdings. His sheep, his equipment, everything."

"He wouldn't accept any such arrangement as that," Manchester said.

Dex's smile was sly. "He will if he thinks his benefactor will be the one holding the note."

Manchester clapped his hands again. "By God, sir, you may have something here. He'll sell out and never know that it's me doing the buying."

"Exactly," Dex said.

"I'll be damned," Clay mumbled. "That could work. If you can talk him into it."

"Oh, I can. I'm sure of that," Dex said. "Can you take care of the legal niceties, Mr. Clay?"

"Easily," Clay said.

"How long will it take for your part of the plan?" Dex asked.

Clay shrugged. "A few days. That's all. I'll draw up the transfer of water rights and the mortgage papers. That will take no more than two . . . let's call it three days at the most. This is something I shall have to do with my own hand, you understand. I wouldn't trust a clerk or amanuensis with these documents. Better I do it myself."

"Excellent idea," Manchester said with enthusiasm. "Best to get cracking on it, Ambrose m'boy. You can leave after dinner and start work on the papers as soon as you get back to town, eh?"

"But I thought—"

"I know, I know. I promised you a night with Dollethra. Haven't forgotten that. Not at all. But this is important, don't you see. Best you get cracking on it straight-away."

Dex almost felt sorry for the poor son of a bitch. He didn't know who Dollethra was. But Brose Clay certainly did. His disappointment was palpable.

"Another time, Ambrose," Manchester said. "I'll not forget your sacrifice. Do what I need and I shall reward you well." He chuckled. "Might even give you Dollethra for your own. What would you say to that?"

The offer seemed enough to mollify Clay. Almost.

Manchester cackled and clapped a little more, then said, "We'll celebrate with squab and oysters, eh Clay? Build up your stamina for Dollethra, right?"

"Right, sir."

Manchester turned and led the way out of the library and down the hall into the dining room where everything was laid in readiness. Dex suspected there would've been hell to pay if the meal hadn't been ready when Manchester decided to eat.

Still, it was a genuinely good meal. And not a single item of Mexican or Spanish cuisine.

◆ 39 ◆

"Good night, Mr. Yancey."

"Good night, Sir David."

"Mind you bolt your door. Wouldn't want some thieving kafir t' come in and slice your purse open, would we?"

Dex was surprised. First that Manchester would admit to any possibility that his servants were trained to anything less than perfection, second because as the now favored hired hand—and he had no doubt whatsoever about where he really stood in Manchester's arrogantly aristocratic estimation—Dexter had more than half expected to be the recipient of a visit from the fabled Dollethra who put poor Clay into such a lather of lustful intent.

Oh, well. He hadn't come out here to get laid. Anita had taken care of that for him last night, thank you. He could wait until he got back out to the Espinosa hacienda. If he had to.

He accepted Manchester's advice and not only bolted his bedroom door, he also made sure the windows were secured and that there was no one lurking in the mahogany wardrobe that occupied nearly one full interior wall in the very large and handsomely appointed guest room.

Dex yawned and stripped to the buff. He hadn't thought to bring clothes for an overnight stay and he would both smell and feel better tomorrow if he did not sleep in his clothing tonight.

He took a leak in the thunder mug—porcelain of a very superior quality, he noted—and replaced the fluids with a swallow of water from the pitcher standing ready on a side table.

He felt more than ready for some sleep after nearly a full day of having to be on his guard against any slip of the tongue while in Manchester's company, so he made short shrift of extinguishing the lamp that had been left burning for him, then crawled between sheets already turned down and pillows fluffed.

The bed felt good. Unusually soft. But very nice. Goose down, he suspected. The sheets smelled of sunshine and soft breezes, and he felt himself drifting into sleep within moments.

Felt that odd, floating sensation that sometimes comes in the final moments before slumber. He let his body go completely loose and limp so that he no longer was aware of his feet, his legs, his arms. He existed only from the neck up so far as external sensation admitted. He could very faintly hear the soft exhalations of his own muted breathing.

Be damned, he mused idly. I snore. But politely. Every so politely.

All sensory experience outside his own limp form faded away until the only things left was—

He blinked.

The only thing left of worldly sense, he realized, was a sense of heat at his midsection.

Ah! A dream. A gentle, lovely dream.

And a rather titillating dream at that.

Goodness, what an excellent imagination he possessed.

He felt as if he were engulfed in something warm and moist. As if his cock had been immersed in body temperature water. Or wax. The sensation was of more substance than water. Wax, he decided. But gracious, what an odd thing to imagine. It wasn't like he was especially horny. Not after last night with Anita.

Probably that was all it was. His imagination was having fun with memories of Anita. It felt almost exactly like this when Anita took him into her mouth.

Hell, he would almost swear he could feel that same soft suction.

He was hard now. Despite the nearness of sleep, his cock reacted to the make-believe suction and the tickling flow of make-believe saliva.

He became hard as a kiln-fired brick and damn near as hot.

The suction slipped for a moment, and he heard a startlingly loud intake of breath.

That was no fucking imaginary noise, Dex realized with a start.

He sat bolt upright in the feather-soft bed and reached beneath the bedcovers to find his hand resting on the back of a very real head.

"Who the hell—"

Dex heard soft laughter and then in the nearly complete dark of the bedroom he saw pale hints of white. Grinning teeth and a pair of catlike eyes.

"Dollethra," he said. It wasn't really a question.

The answer was in that same clicketty-clack tongue that conveyed no meaning to him.

But then the truth was that Dollethra needed no English. Not for this. This she could communicate just fine without words, thank you.

·40·

Dex stood, his limbs with no more strength or substance to them than if they'd been formed from bits of wet cloth, and shakily fumbled on the bedside table for the silver box he'd seen there before extinguishing the lamp. He found the object, managed after several failed attempts to get the lid open and found the matches he was looking for inside.

He had no idea where the striker might be so leaned down and scraped the match head across the floor. On his third try the match flamed up and he was able to light the lamp.

"Good Lord!" he muttered when he saw the woman. She was as black as a lump of coal and had a body that looked like it was carved from shiny anthracite.

She was tall, he saw, with no discernible body fat anywhere on her. Even her chest was rock hard and as flat as a man's.

This was no man, though. Dex knew that, for he'd already enjoyed the pleasures of her three times. And that was not counting that first time in her mouth.

He'd never before seen a woman so muscular and sculptured. Oddly, that did not in the least make her any the less feminine. Nor did the fact that her tightly curly hair was cropped as close as a . . . sheep's wool was the first thought that came to mind. It was hardly the best choice, given place and circumstance. But it fit. Her hair was clipped so close it looked like a knit cap pulled tight over her skull.

Even so she was every bit feminine, every inch desirable.

"How tall are you," he asked. He could not tell that for himself while she lay curled deep within the feather mattress—where she'd been hiding, already in the bed and concealed underneath the covers before Dex ever entered the room and locked himself so securely inside—but he had the impression Dollethra was tall as well as lean.

She tilted her head and gave him a feline smile but did not answer.

"Stand up for a minute would you, please?"

She smiled and turned a little, moving and posing as if a statue come newly to life. She showed herself to him and motioned toward her pussy, which she'd shaved as bald as an infant's. Not that it made her look like a child. Hardly that. But it was . . . interesting. One could damn sure say that. The sight of a bare naked pussy was really quite intriguing.

"Do you speak English?"

Dollethra said something to him. The words sounded like bones rattling together inside an empty keg. She pointed first to herself and then to Dex's limp and exhausted pecker.

He shook his head. "Sorry," he said. "It's all used up. Got to rest for a while first."

Dollethra pointed again. First to him, then to herself.

"Cannot do," Dex told her. Not that she understood.

The beautiful woman—and she was most definitely, most stunningly beautiful—moved toward him with all the elegant grace of a stalking lioness.

"I really can't," Dex said. "I'm used up for now. Really."

Dollethra smiled. And leaned forward.

He could feel her breath warm on shriveled, wrinkled, overused skin.

Dollethra reached up and with the palm of her hand mimed for Dex to close his eyes. He did.

For several seconds he felt nothing.

And then he felt . . . everything.

Warm. Wet. All over. His prick. His balls. She guided him gently around so that he faced away from her. He felt her hands at his crotch, as soft as her lips and tongue had been. And—the sensations were incredible—felt the probing of her tongue around and around and into his asshole.

It wasn't possible. Really it wasn't. But within seconds Dex was hard again and eager to enter this exotic creature one more time.

No wonder that son of a bitch Clay wanted to spend the night here instead of bent over a desk in his office back in town.

No wonder Clay would do just damn near anything for the promise of a night with Dollethra.

Lordy, he thought, as she eased him down onto the bed and, straddling him, began to lavish sensations on him that he'd never dreamed possible.

• 41 •

It was the middle of the next morning before Dex dragged himself out of the sweaty, rumpled, much enjoyed bed.

Dollethra had slipped away at some time during the night. By that point Dexter was almost glad to see her go. Much more of her pumping and pounding and she would have killed him. Of course he would have died happy. But even so . . .

He went downstairs and was greeted by the same exquisite black girl who'd escorted him in yesterday. Manchester might be a real son of a bitch, Dex thought, but the man certainly had good taste when it came to women.

"The master said you should have breakfast before you go. Do you remember the way to the dining room?"

"Yes, thank you. Will Sir David be joining me?"

"Oh, no. The master left early this morning. There were some things he wanted to do. Is this a problem, sir?"

"No, not at all."

"I will have your horse washed and saddled, sir. It will be ready for you by the time you leave."

Dex thanked her again and made his way back to the dining room where a pair of dusky young women waited, ready to take his breakfast requests.

He looked at them now in a different manner than he had yesterday. James used to tease him sometimes about Dex's reluctance to bed black girls. Dollethra had been a first for him. Now . . . hell, he knew every black girl couldn't be as outstandingly good in the feathers as Dollethra. Of course not.

But he couldn't help but think about the depths of pleasure she'd given him when now he looked at these other, albeit less stunning young women.

When Dex saw James again—if Dex saw James again—he didn't honestly know if he would admit this truly incredible experience to his oldest and dearest friend. Maybe so. Or not.

Dex filled up on baking powder biscuits and creamy sausage gravy, then polished off half a pot of coffee. By the time he was done he felt halfway human again and had regained enough stamina that he thought he could manage to walk out and climb onto his horse without falling flat on his face.

Even so, he was secretly pleased that the boy with the steps was there to help him into the saddle.

He thanked the kid even though he was fairly sure not a word of it would be understood, then wheeled the animal around and headed down the road leading away from the Victoria Cross headquarters. A mile or so out he reined to a halt and sat there for a moment trying to work out in his mind the physical relationships between Manchester's ranch, Huaca Guadalupe, and the Espinosa hacienda.

At length, not exactly positive of the direction he wanted but believing he had the general idea of it, he turned off the road and started out cross-country.

· 42 ·

He saw the buzzards first but really didn't pay much attention to them. Just more dead sheep, he figured. Since leaving the Victoria Cross he'd probably ridden past fifty or more of the decaying carcasses, yet by actual count saw only four live sheep. And those were gaunt and scrawny, seeming more dead than alive even while they still stood.

The buzzards were circling high above a rocky mound. Dex didn't have any desire to see more dead things so intended to skirt the base of the mound and stay well clear of the dying ground.

That was until he saw the horses tied to some greasewood on the north side of the craggy hill. Dex frowned and drew rein. Those horses looked familiar. He turned his animal and started up toward the top.

"Afternoon, boys," he said when he reached the summit to find Ben Turlock there, along with his shadows Big and Bigger.

"Afternoon yourself, mister," Turlock said. He did not sound particularly friendly. But then he wouldn't, Dex supposed. Not after that little dispute they'd had the other day.

"You're too late," Big said. Dex couldn't remember the asshole's actual name. Didn't care to either.

"Too late for what?" Dex asked.

He looked around. The men were standing inside a natural redoubt overlooking the Espinosa hacienda. The adobe walls were half a mile or so to the south and probably several hundred feet lower in elevation than this vantage point.

A brass spyglass lying atop a flat rock showed that this was where Clay had posted his men so as to keep an eye on the comings and goings at the rancho.

"Too late for some pussy," Big gloated.

"Shut up, Ev. Shut your fucking mouth."

Turlock's advice, of course, was too late. Just like Big claimed Dexter was.

"What pussy d'you mean?" Dex asked, his voice calm and as close to being friendly as he could manage.

"Meskin woman," Big cackled.

"What Mexican woman?" Dex asked.

"Keep your yap shut, Ev," Turlock warned.

"Oh hell, Ben. He's on our side, ain't he? 'Sides, done is done. The bitch went an' died. Can't change that now, can we?"

"What the hell are you two talking about?" Dex asked.

Turlock gave Gardner a warning look, and Big belatedly hushed up. Dex stepped down from his horse and took a look around.

There was no fire ring, of course. The watchers wouldn't be able to light a fire up here without drawing attention to themselves. Probably they maintained a camp somewhere close by where they could cook and eat. Up here at the top of the tor he could see only some bits of trash scattered on the ground, some rifles stacked haphazardly against a rock and over there some dirty clothes dropped carelessly onto the ground.

Except . . . Dex's breath caught, and a sick, empty feeling clutched at his belly.

That was no bundle of rags lying on the ground in the shadow of one of the taller rocks. It was a body. Or was it?

He shot an ugly glance in the direction of the three men and walked over to the motionless figure.

It was a woman. A dark-haired Mexican woman. Dex couldn't tell if he'd seen her down at the hacienda over the past few days. She'd been battered so badly that her face was disfigured to the point that he could not be certain what she might have looked like in life.

Life, however, was most assuredly gone from her now. She'd been stripped naked and raped until the insides of her thighs were crusted with blood.

The most terrible thing was not that, though. Her chest was . . . missing. The sons of bitches had cut the dead woman's tits off.

"What the hell did you do that for?" Dex demanded of them.

"Do what?"

"That!" He pointed.

It was Bigger who answered. "We cut 'em off, o' course. What the hell d' you think?"

"Why?"

"T'baccy pouches, that's why. My uncle was in the Colorado Volunteers 'way back when. He was there when they whupped shit outa Black Kettle an' his Cheyennes. My uncle had him a pouch made from the titty skin o' a Injun squaw. Now I can make me a pouch, too. His had the purtiest li'l shriveled up nipple on the bottom o' the bag. Think this will shrink up when it dries, mister?" Bigger laughed and pulled a red-smeared scrap of limp flesh from his pocket.

Dex looked at it and felt a wave of dizziness. For a moment he thought he was going to puke.

"Put that away, Artie," Turlock grumbled.

"I can't believe you did this," Dex said. But of course he could believe it. He had to. He could see it. Jesus, God!

Turlock shrugged. "She was just a fucking Meskin. They're no better than Injuns anyhow."

"What did you do, go down and kidnap her?"

"Naw. Mr. Clay told us not to cause no ruckus, just to keep watch. But that woman, she came wandering up here looking for . . . hell, I dunno what she was looking for. Yarbs or flowers or some damn thing. Doesn't matter. She walked right up here and seen us. So what was we to do, I ask you. Let her fucking go back and tell the rest of the greasers that we been up here watching them? So we had us a little fun with her. Didn't mean for her to die, necessarily. That just sorta happened. You know?"

"What I know," Dex said, "is that you bastards are going to hang. For murder. I'll see to that, damn you."

"You'll *what*?"

"You heard me. I'm turning you in to the law. Count on it."

"The hell you say, mister. You ain't turning nobody in to Johnny Law. Nobody."

"Just watch me."

Dex heard the clatter of a carbine lever being worked and turned to see Big with a rifle in his hands, the muzzle aimed dead on Dex's belt buckle. "We don't figure to hang, mister."

"Shoot the sonuvabitch, Ev," Turlock said.

"No, Ev, wait up a minute," Bigger said. "My head's still sore as a fucking boil from where this bastard snuck up an' clonked me th' other day. Don't you go shooting him just yet. I want to beat on him some first."

"Take that gun off your belt, mister," Big said. He laughed. "Drop your pistol an' we'll give you a chance." The laughter grew louder. "All you got t' do, mister is whip Art in a fair fight an' we'll give you a running start. Fifty yard start, hey? Can't ask better'n that, now can you?"

All three of the plug-uglies seemed to think that was an uproariously amusing suggestion.

"The gun, mister. Right fucking now or I'll pull this trigger an' my pal Artie won't be able to have his fun."

Dex's hand began to move.

"Slow, mister, an' careful. The left hand an' just two fingers. Easy now. That's nice."

Dex did as he was told. Slow and careful. Two fingers only. The heavy Webley hit the ground with a thump. Dex would have been satisfied had it gone off and put a bullet into one of the threesome, but it did not. The damned thing just bounced once and lay there.

"That's nice," Big said. He uncocked the Winchester and laid it aside.

Bigger flexed the muscles on arms that looked the size of a horse's thigh.

"Well, shit!" Dex complained. The expression did not generate any sympathy among the three men though, and without bothering to take time to remove his shirt Bigger started forward with his hands balled into massive, hairy fists.

"Shit," Dex repeated. And sighed loud enough for the men to hear.

◆ 43 ◆

Bigger had a very happy and eager look on his broad face. He still had it when Dex reached beneath his coat to the small of his back and drew the other Webley.

He took careful aim and shot Bigger in the forehead, swiveled quickly to his right and again took time to place his shot with care. Big was leaning over reaching for the Winchester. Dex put a 255 grain lead slug through the man's left temple.

Before Big's body had time enough to hit the ground Dex was dropping into a crouch and spinning to his left, toward Ben Turlock.

Turlock was in a state of shock. Both his companions were down and dead in little more than an eyeblink of time, and now he found himself peering into the gaping, smoky muzzle of a very large revolver.

Apparently it was quite all right for Turlock and his chums to rape and slaughter. But the son of a bitch didn't seem to think it at all fair that the tables might be turned, that their next intended victim might have the audacious effrontery to actually fight back.

Turlock threw his hands high and dropped to his knees. "It was them, Mr. Yancey, it was only them," he shrieked.

Dex was sure the man was reaching for a concealed weapon of some sort.

At least that's what Dex told himself afterward.

The thought came to him just after he shot Ben Turlock square on the bridge of the man's nose.

Turlock's head snapped back and he stayed like that for long seconds, on his knees, his thick torso swaying.

Then he toppled forward face down onto the sharp gravel and hard stone of the hilltop.

Funny, Dex thought, how a body nearly always falls face first no matter how hard the killing blow or from what direction it came. A dead man falls forward regardless.

Funny. Right. Real funny.

Wearily Dex bent and retrieved the other Webley and returned it to his belly holster. Then he broke open the number two gun and reloaded it.

He felt numb. Not proud of what he'd done here, certainly. Not even particularly pleased by it. He just felt . . . numb.

After a time he walked over to the mutilated dead woman. He considered retrieving . . . no, dammit. That would be going just too far with this. He didn't want to touch the trophy skin in Bigger's pocket. Didn't want to touch Bigger either if it came to that.

He settled for walking downhill to where the dead men's horses were tied so he could fetch back a blanket and wrap the woman in it.

Turlock and Gardner and Broyle didn't deserve that much consideration. Fuck them, one and all.

⋄ 44 ⋄

Dex was beat. Half the day had sped by and he was dead tired. Well, not as dead as some others in the vicinity. But plenty worn out and that was for damned sure.

He'd spent the past hours dragging small rocks up the hill—why there weren't any at the top he didn't know—so he could cover the bodies of Ambrose Clay's late but unlamented bully-boy force.

He hadn't done that out of any sort of respect. Rather the labor was required in order to hide the deaths. He didn't want anything to interfere with his plan to double cross Sir David Francis Manchester.

Clay might assume Turlock and company were still out here on duty if they simply failed to show up. But if bodies were found it would only throw a wrench into the gears of the progress Dex was making, especially if Manchester blamed the Espinosas for the killings and decided to retaliate.

No, Dex figured, it would be for the best if the three men just disappeared.

As for any remorse on his part, there wasn't a smidgen to be found. These were assuredly the same men who'd murdered those Espinosa sheepherders, and a rock cairn atop a windswept hill was more than any of them deserved. The hell with them.

Dex finished with that chore, then led one of the horses up to the Mexican woman's body so he could load that across the saddle. She deserved a decent burial and her family's tears, and he intended to see that she got them.

Finally, remounted and leading all three horses, he moved slowly down the hill with the afternoon sunlight slanting low to his right. With luck he should reach the hacienda before nightfall.

"Estelle will bring water for your bath, Dexter. A meal is being prepared now. Do you want to eat before you wash or after?"

"After," he said. Perhaps by then he'd have an appetite again. At the moment he was just too tired to care about food even though he hadn't eaten since breakfast back at the Victoria Cross.

"Will I . . . see you later?" he asked after a moment of awkward silence.

"Perhaps," Anita told him.

"You'll tell your grandfather everything I told you?" he pressed.

She nodded. "I will speak with him. I can make you no promise more. You un'erstan' me so?"

"I understand that, yes," Dex told her.

"Then wait here. The tub and water will be brought soon."

Anita hurried away. Out in the compound Dex could hear the mournful wailing and loudly uttered prayers of the dead woman's family. They had identified her, although only God knew how, considering the condition she was in after those men were done with her.

Dex was not in the Espinosas' own home now but in a small and long empty place that might once have housed servants or the family of a sheepherder. Perhaps, Dex thought, this had been the home of one of the sheepherders killed by Turlock and his men.

The house was not even built of the sturdy adobe but of cruder material. Thin saplings had been placed upright and lined tight together in a ditch, then tied at the top by weaving even smaller saplings around and through the upper ends. Light timbers were laid from one wall to another to act as rafters and a roof laid up from twigs and clumps of sod. The walls were plastered inside and out with mud that had hardened and formed a rather shiny surface. Someone—Ambrose Clay perhaps?—had told him that manure was added to ordinary mud to make the durable brown plaster.

No matter. It didn't smell now that it was dry, and in this climate the structure apparently lasted for a long time between repairs.

A wooden bunk with bare slats and an empty ticking sack folded at the head was against one wall. A single stool was provided for the comfort of the occupant, and there was a mud fireplace built into a back corner. Pegs inserted into the walls on either side of the door would serve as wardrobe and storage facilities. There were no other furnishings.

This was, Dex thought, a far cry from the sumptuous quarters he'd been given last night at Victoria Cross.

It hurt him, dammit, that he was not even permitted inside the Espinosa family residence now.

He'd gone far out of his way to help these people and he . . . aw, shit! He was feeling sorry for himself, wasn't he? What a useless and stupid exercise that was. Always was.

Old Don Cesar had been offended. Dex had screwed both the old man's granddaughters—and for that matter would cheerfully do it again if he had the chance—and to a stiff-necked aristocrat like the don, that was a grievous thing indeed.

Minor retaliations like being shown out through a servant's entrance and now being denied access to the family dining room really didn't matter all that much, Dex realized.

Certainly he was not going to dash off in a fit of pique and neglect to do what he could to help. Right was still right and wrong was still wrong and never mind the picky, petty details. Dexter Lee Yancey would do what he thought was right and proper, and that was the end of that.

He took a seat on the three-legged stool and leaned back against the cow shit wall to wait for Anita or whoever else might want to drop by this evening.

◆ 45 ◆

Four days later it still rankled that that old son of a bitch Don Cesar whatever-whatever Espinosa wouldn't allow him into the house. But it bothered Dex's sense of propriety even more that an asshole like David Manchester would think he could come to this country and get away with murder.

If the guy thought he should be allowed to hold the power of life and death over the peasantry then let him go back to his own country and try it.

Dex was contemplating those and other things over a beer when a boy—a red-headed Anglo kid with freckles—came to find him.

"You're Mr. Yancey, ain't you?"

"That's right."

"Mr. Clay said I should tell you he has some papers for you to sign. Whatever that means."

"That means you've brought me some very good news," Dex said. He picked up his change from the bar—

thirty five cents in silver—and handed it to the kid.
"Thanks."

"Gee, mister, thank *you*." The boy went racing away to
report his good fortune. Probably to his pals, Dex thought.
He wouldn't be running so fast if he was just going to
hand the windfall over to his mama.

Dex took a last swallow of his beer and left the rest of
it sitting on the bar when he walked out into the mid-day
sunlight and headed for the bank building.

He'd never been inside Ambrose Clay's office, but he
had no trouble finding it. It was an unpretentious little
alcove at the back of the bank building with a separate
entrance and a small, hand-lettered sign announcing A. M.
Clay, Attorney at Law.

Dex let himself in without bothering to knock.

"Ah. I see you got my message."

"I did. You have the papers ready?"

"Indeed. I took them out to the ranch last night."

"Spend the night there, did you?" Dex asked with a
knowing grin.

"God, she's good, isn't she," Clay exclaimed.

At least there was that one thing he and Clay agreed
about, Dex thought. "You won't find any better." Dex
returned to the principal subject at hand. "Everything is
signed and ready for me to show the old man? You know
Don Cesar won't entrust his water rights to me if I can't
prove that I already hold Sir David's free and clear."

"Oh, yes. With these papers, Yancey, you have control
over practically every water right for sixty miles west and
a good twenty miles to the east of here. And a fifty mile
swath north and south. Not the land itself, of course. But
the water, and it's the water that makes the land useable.

Now all you need are the matching documents from Espinosa."

"You have those ready?"

Clay nodded. "Right here. Get him to sign them, and the deed is done." He laughed. "That was a pun, you see."

"Was it? I hadn't noticed."

Clay scowled. Then in a burst of enthusiasm seemed to forgive Dexter all his transgressions. He laughed again. Dex began to wonder just what marvels the lawyer had been promised as his part of the reward. And thinking of which—

"You have something for me other than the documents, I believe?"

"Yes, of course. Can't forget that, can we?"

"Not if Sir David wants this to happen, we can't," Dex agreed.

Clay crossed his office to a filing cabinet and removed a small leather folio. He brought it to Dex and handed it over. "In currency, not gold, just as you requested. With a most generous bonus, I might add. Sir David is, shall we say, extremely good to his friends."

Dex smiled. "I was counting on that."

"Yes, well, there's four thousand cash there. You're welcome to count it if you wish."

"Brose. Hey! I trust you."

"Yes, well, um . . . the documents. Where did I put the rest of the documents? And I'll want you to pay close attention now. Everything has to be signed in the don's own hand and with his name in full. And of course you'll need two witnesses. You can act as one witness. The other can be a family member. Or I could ride out with you and sign as the second witness."

"That won't be necessary," Dex said. "We don't want

to arouse any suspicions, you know, or make the old man uncomfortable."

"No, I'd not want to jeopardize everything now that we have it as good as in hand."

"Exactly."

Dex patiently waited through a boring twenty minutes in which Clay explained to him over and over and endlessly over again exactly where and how each conveyance was to be signed and where the witnesses should attest to the validity of the signatures.

Not that any of these documents would ever be signed by anyone.

What Dex wanted was already in his possession, already signed by Manchester.

Once Dex handed them to Don Cesar—or more likely to Anita since the old bastard still wouldn't consent to permit Dex within his sacred walls—Don Cesar would have control over everything David Manchester had established here.

Well, not the livestock, of course. Manchester would still have his cows and his mansion. He just wouldn't be able to water the cows. Or turn a profit from the mansion and the now useless Victoria Cross grazing leaseholds.

It was, Dex thought, a rather satisfying outcome.

"Thank you, Brose. You're a gentleman and a scholar." Not that Dex meant either term. Clay beamed anyway and shook Dex's hand with vigor.

"Will you ride out to see Espinosa today?"

"Yes, right away."

Probably the sensible thing for him to do, Dex considered, would be to first go back to the hotel and pack all his things. He could drop these papers off at the hacienda and ride on to Santa Fe.

On the other hand, dammit, Clay might hear about it if Dex cleared out. It wouldn't be too late for something to go wrong.

No, he decided, it would be safer if he left town straight from the lawyer's office. He could come back in the morning—although the prospect of another night on that hard-as-stone bunk in the jacale was not an inviting one—and get his things.

That would be much better.

"Good luck, Yancey."

Dex smiled at him. "The hard part is all done, you know. From here it's only a downriver float." Not that he expected a lawyer from this nearly waterless country to fully understand that. But who cared what Ambrose Clay did or did not comprehend.

Dex didn't have to worry about that at all any longer.

"G'bye, Brose."

"Good-bye, Yancey."

Dex let himself out of the office and headed direct to the livery where his horse was quartered.

· 46 ·

"Well, shit!" Dex grumbled. It probably wasn't yet eight o'clock in the morning and already his day was ruined.

He'd intended to ride quietly into Huaca Guadalupe, pack his things and get the hell out of town before anyone was the wiser. It wasn't going to be like that. At the same time Dex reached the outskirts of town from one direction, so did Sir David Manchester, coming in from the other way.

Manchester, with Ambrose Clay seated beside him on the soft cushions of a fancy landau, seemed extremely pleased to see Dexter.

Dex for his part of it was not at all enthused with the prospect of facing the little man who he'd just gulled out of a potential fortune. Ill-gotten perhaps but a fortune nonetheless.

Dammit.

Manchester said something to his driver, and the team

was pulled to a halt so Manchester could stand upright—likely was afraid he'd topple out and land head first in the dirt if he tried to stand while the rig was in motion—and quite grandly motion for Dexter to come nigh.

For reasons known only to God and himself, today Manchester had chosen to deck himself out in a full and quite gaudy military uniform.

Hussars, Dex guessed, with a shiny chromium helmet, red and gold ostrich plumes, golden epaulet shoulder boards, bright red tunic, intensely white breaches, and some handsome but dreadfully hot and heavy cavalry boots that came well above the knee and had to be supported there with elastic garters.

The man was even wearing a saber with a huge basketlike hand guard and gold tassels. Incredible.

Dex guessed that Manchester was feeling quite full of himself now and—quite mistakenly of course—considered himself to now be the emperor of all northeastern New Mexico Territory.

In a way, Dex realized, it wasn't an altogether bad thing that he'd run into Manchester this way.

Now he would have the pleasure of informing the little prick in person that his dreams were dashed and shot to hell. The water now belonged to the Espinosas. All of the water. And even as they spoke a rider was carrying the documents to Don Cesar's political allies in Santa Fe for recording with the territorial governor. The courier left late last night with the pouch of documents Ambrose Clay drew up and Manchester himself signed and certified.

By now, with the courier a good eight or nine hours on his way, there was nothing Manchester could do to stop the process.

Dex wheeled his horse about and rode to meet Manchester on the main street of Huaca Guadalupe.

· 47 ·

"You . . . did . . . what?"

Manchester had gone instantly pale at the news Dex gave him. The man was aghast. His mouth gaped like a fish taking in nothing but insubstantial air. "You . . . you . . . couldn't have."

"Wrong," Dex said cheerfully. "I could and I did. You're out of the cow business, Manchester old fellow. I would suggest to you that you also take yourself out of this territory. Hell, while you're at it, take yourself out of the United States. We don't need any more of your kind. We have enough home-grown assholes. No point in importing more of them."

"I'll . . . I'll—"

"You'll do shit, that's what you'll do, Manchester," Dex said, warming up to this now that it was started. "If you do try to do anything more, y'see, I intend to write some letters. My family has influence in Washington City, by the way." They didn't. But Manchester wouldn't know that.

"I'll write some letters to certain cabinet members there. And others to . . . let me see now." He pulled a sheet of paper from his pocket, unfolded it, and looked it over for a moment before continuing. "Let me see here. We have a James Edgarson of Brestwick. Wherever that is. And Earl Bedford of Clive." Dex paused for a moment to look over the top of the sheet at an even paler Manchester. "Is Earl the man's name or a title?" He shrugged. "No matter. Let me see who else we have here."

He inspected the paper again. "Really, though, there's no point in reading off these names. You already know them all. Your investors."

"How . . . how—?"

"On the deeds you conveyed to Don Cesar, Sir David. Your investors were listed as partners in the landholdings. I took the liberty of jotting down their names. Thought they might want to know how their money has been managed over here in the wild wilds of North America. I rather suspect they don't know all the, shall we say, finer points of your stewardship. Perhaps they should, eh?"

"You . . . my God, man, you've ruined me."

"Yes," Dex said cheerfully, "I daresay that I have indeed ruined you, Manchester. And a finer candidate for it I couldn't have found, thank you."

"I'm . . . my father . . . my friends—"

"Do they know you claim to've won the V.C.?" Dex asked. "Bet they'd like to know that, too."

That shot was, he quickly realized, too telling for Manchester to take.

Losing money, even criminally mishandling it, the upper crust British gentlemen back home in jolly aulde England might have been able to swallow and to forgive if not exactly forget.

But for a gentleman, a purported gentleman, to claim honors he'd not earned . . . that they would never forgive. Everything else, yes. But not that.

With an anguished, gut-wrenching cry, Manchester dragged his saber from its scabbard and charged Dex with the heavy blade upraised.

• 48 •

Dex abandoned his saddle a split second before Manchester's saber slashed onto the place where Dexter's thigh had been a moment before. Dex threw himself off to the right, scrambled to his feet, and was able to pluck his cane from the boot where he carried it slung on the saddle.

Dex's horse quite naturally believed itself to be the object of the assault and did the sensible thing. It let out one quick snort of terror and departed at a high rate of speed, leaving nothing between Dexter and an enraged Manchester but a few feet of New Mexico soil and a very slender malacca cane.

Dex twisted the eaglesbeak handle and pulled to expose his own sword. Of course his cane sword was at least four inches shorter than Manchester's saber and its blade weighed probably a quarter what Manchester's did.

Manchester leaped forward again with an overhand

sweep of his saber. Dex darted to the side, and Manchester's blow cut only air.

"Damn you!" Manchester sounded close to tears. Close hell; Dex was pretty sure there really were tears welling up in the insanely furious fellow's eyes.

Fine. Let 'em blind the bastard. Dex wasn't so sporting as to give him time to dry his eyes.

Manchester wasn't blind yet, dammit. He came pressing forward again and again, leading with his right boot, stomping the ground forcefully with each advance, slashing time after time in those overhand blows any one of which would split a man's skull in two if the blade were to connect.

If it did. Dex kept moving back. Sideways. Back. To the other side. Manchester kept coming on.

Dex's automatic reaction was to block the blows and parry with his own sword. He stopped himself. His light blade would be shattered if Manchester's saber ever once chopped down onto it.

Manchester stepped forward. Slashed. Stepped forward.

Dexter dodged and weaved and wished Manchester's arm would give out. That was one heavy son of a bitch of a saber he was swinging. Surely he couldn't keep this up indefinitely.

On the other hand, dammit, he didn't have to swing the thing the whole day long. All he needed to do was connect once and once only, and that would put an end to the fight.

Dex backed away again and again until he came up against the low fence that surrounded Pancho's cafe. He could retreat no further. He could—

He could quit being such an idiot, he realized. He'd

been playing Manchester's game. Letting the saber dictate the terms of the combat.

That was wrong.

Manchester's training was with the saber. Broad strokes swinging and slashing.

But Dexter's blade was more like that of the epee. He could cut with it, true, but its best use was not to cut but to thrust.

And a saber man, even an expert swordsman with that heavy weapon, is vulnerable to the thrust.

Dex ducked underneath a backhanded swipe of Manchester's saber.

But this time instead of darting away again, Dex stepped forward. He stepped *into* Manchester's attack not away from it.

Manchester's eyes widened as perhaps he too realized the importance of what Dex had done.

If so he knew it only for a moment or two, because the point of Dex's sword jabbed unerringly into Manchester's throat just beneath the shelf of the little man's jaw.

Blood made frothy with a sudden exhalation of breath poured down the front of Manchester's uniform and blended too well with the scarlet of his tunic.

The man looked at Dex for a moment and then, oddly, raised his saber, blade sideways, and touched the hilt to his forehead in a silent salute.

Then Manchester's knees buckled, and he toppled face forward into the dry, sun-baked dust of the street.

· 49 ·

Dex met another carriage on his way out of town. This one was a much older and far less elegant rig, but there had been a time when it would have been considered quite grand.

Dex drew rein to allow the carriage to pass, but he made no effort to approach it. A young man he recognized from the hacienda was driving. He could see Anita and Anselma in the back, both dressed to the nines with their hair piled high beneath lacy mantillas.

He hadn't seen Anselma in days, and last night he'd only been allowed to converse with Anita while in the company of a duena who acted as chaperon. He gathered that both were under strict orders to avoid him. He didn't want to cause them any further trouble with their grandfather so he sat where he was—a little uncomfortable because of the gash in the leather seat of his saddle where Manchester's first saber stroke landed—and doffed his hat respectfully.

The carriage too came to a halt. The door swung open, and old Don Cesar emerged.

Dex quickly dismounted. It would have been disrespectful for him to remain physically higher than the don. Of course Dex was a good head taller than Don Cesar, but he couldn't do anything about that, short of kneeling, and there was no way he intended to do that.

He did, however, bow just a little as the old man approached him.

Don Cesar stood in silence for long moments, looking Dex over from head to foot and back again until Dex began to feel extremely uncomfortable. What did the old fart want now? Dex had done everything he could for him. As for the girls, well, he couldn't take that back now if he wanted to. And wouldn't have even if he'd had the power to turn the clock back. They were nice girls and he hadn't taken anything from them that they did not freely offer. He had no regrets about that, never mind what their grandfather might think.

Dex considered trying to explain. But there was no point in it. Don Cesar would think and do what he chose. That was up to him. Dex had acted in a way he believed to be honorable. He wasn't going to worry beyond that.

After a good minute and a half of silent scrutiny, the wizened but intensely proud old man abruptly nodded . . . and thrust a hand forward.

His hand felt like so many brittle twigs, but the grip was firm and uncompromising.

He shook Dexter's hand without a word, then turned and walked back to his carriage.

The driver waited for Don Cesar to enter, then turned the carriage around, and spanked the team into a fast trot back in the direction of the hacienda.

"Well, I'll be a son of a bitch," Dex breathed. "The old bastard forgave me."

Dex felt good, very good in fact, when he bumped his horse into a walk and then into a smooth extended walk.

Santa Fe lay somewhere ahead. And God knew what else.